01/10

W9-BUT-894

the Blonde of the Joke

the Blonde of the Joke

BENNETT MADISON

An Imprint of HarperCollins*Publishers*

HarperTeen is an imprint of HarperCollins Publishers.

The Blonde of the Joke
Copyright © 2009 by Bennett Madison

www.harperteen.com
Library of Congress Cataloging-in-Publication Data
Madison, Bennett.
The blonde of the joke / Bennett Madison. — 1st ed.
      p.   cm.
Summary: A mousy brunette who goes unnoticed at her high school discovers
that she has a sneaky, wild side when she teams up with a flashy blonde classmate
to shoplift from upscale stores in the local mall.
ISBN 978-0-06-125560-1 (trade bdg.)
[1. Shoplifting—Fiction. 2. Stealing—Fiction. 3. Friendship—Fiction.] I. Title.
PZ7.M26Bl 2008   2008005797
[Fic]—dc22   CIP
                                                                             AC
Typography by Michelle Gengaro-Kokmen

09 10 11 12 13   CG/RRDB   10 9 8 7 6 5 4 3 2 1
❖
First Edition

For Margaret Gopi Wright

ACKNOWLEDGMENTS

Many thanks are in order:

To my agent, Cathy Hemming, for forcing me to set my sights higher and for making good on every impossible promise.

To my editor, Tara Weikum, for gentle guidance, invaluable criticism, boundless faith, and, most importantly, for getting the joke.

To Jocelyn Davies, for her enthusiasm—and for that check.

To Bob Berens, for being the world's smartest reader.

To James Freedland, for focus.

To Alice Wetterlund, for makeup tips.

To the Blondes: Katie Van Wert, Emily Gould, Megan Rogers, Kristin Hagar, Nicole Cloutier, Chloe Honum, Erin McMonagle. For inspiration.

To Elise Broach and Natalie Standiford, for the gossip and advice.

To everyone at the Natural Resources Defense Council, especially Sandy Kolakowski and Milagro Suarez, for being good bosses and for saving the environment.

To my parents, for being patient for twenty-five years.

To Laird Adamson, for everything.

Chapter One

A blonde and a brunette walk into a bar. No, wait.

A blonde and a brunette show up at the Pearly Gates, and Saint Peter—no, not that one, either.

Okay, so a blonde and a brunette go to the mall, and . . . oh, forget it.

If there's one thing I've learned lately, it's that jokes are not funny. At least, they're never funny in the way they're meant to be. I once knew a girl who thought all jokes were funny, but it turned out she was laughing at the wrong parts. Sometimes, now, I wonder what it must be like to look at the world that way. To be able to ignore one punch line and see a different one where it never even existed. I mean, I guess it must be useful. I guess it must be beautiful.

Okay, here we go. Knock-knock. Who's there? Ima. Ima who?

Ima gonna tell you a joke. Get ready to laugh; this one's a good one. Kind of long, but funny. Of course, by funny I mean that it's fucking tragic in the end. Bear with me. It's the first day of school, and a blonde walks into a classroom. . . .

It had been at least ten minutes since the second bell had rung when a blonde walked into the classroom. It was like this: Ms. Tinker was up at the blackboard, halfway through Classroom Policy #3—*No Foolishness*—when the door slammed open and this girl just came sauntering in. This insane-looking girl—all breeze and smiles in a baggy, lime green raincoat that hung to her ankles, and like it was no thing at all. Like it was nothing.

Ms. Tinker had already made it clear that she didn't tolerate tardiness. It was right up there in white chalk. *Classroom Policy #1: I Do Not Tolerate TARDINESS.*

Francie Knight couldn't have been expected to know. She'd been tardy for the first two classroom policies, so how could she? Francie just stood in the doorway, digging through her purse while the class sat silent in anticipation. Ms. Tinker turned from the board, clearing her throat. It was that whole slow-burn business. *I Do Not Tolerate TARDINESS.*

The girl still didn't seem to notice she was in trouble. She had found a tube of lip gloss at the bottom of her purse and was thoughtlessly applying a new coat to her already shiny lips. And then, before Ms. Tinker could say anything, lip gloss still in hand, Francie looked up and cut her off with a confident sneer. A grand and haughty toss of her blond, blond ponytail. You could almost see a yellow shimmer lingering around her face when she spoke.

"Sorry I'm late," Francie said. "I had to make a pit stop at the assistant principal's office on my way over. The first day of school and they're already making me wear the whore's raincoat! Can you believe it?" She reached up and pulled the band from her hair. She let her ponytail unfurl at her shoulders in spiraling, perfectly greasy tangles. "Where should I sit?" she asked.

A murmur had started in the room from somewhere around the vicinity of Shana Miller in the third row. *Who is this freak?* Ms. Tinker pushed her little square eyeglasses up on her nose with her ring finger, regarding Francie suspiciously. She fidgeted with the gym whistle on the lanyard around her neck, as if considering whether to sound an alert. But we all knew it was too late, and it was obvious that Ms. Tinker knew it, too. Francie had the situation well in hand. She had won this round.

She spotted an empty desk right next to me, and plopped her purse down.

"Just see me after class," Ms. Tinker grumbled. At least, that's what I have to assume she said, because no one heard her, including me. No one was paying attention to anything except Francie anymore. Francie removed her raincoat and tossed it over the back of the chair. "Like hell if they think

I'm really going to wear this thing," she said, to no one in particular. "Last time I checked, there was such a thing as the First Amendment in this country." And then I saw why she had called it "the whore's raincoat." Because when she stripped it off, Francie revealed that she was wearing an aqua tube top, a pair of gold lamé hot pants, and the highest heels I had ever seen.

The room was quiet. I looked over at Shana Miller. She was staring, but her face was blank, like she had been hypnotized. Francie had no backpack or notebook; she sat and drummed her long, hot-pink fingernails on her desk, all, *let's get this show on the road*.

"Classroom Policy Number Four," Ms. Tinker sighed. I guess she'd been teaching long enough to know when to give up the fight. She turned back to the board and began to write again. *There Is No Such Thing as a Smart Question.*

Francie giggled. She turned to me and rolled her eyes. I looked away. I felt myself diminished just from sitting next to her. My shoulders crumpled into my rib cage. I couldn't look at her. But I couldn't not look at her, either.

Francie was that kind of girl. You know the type I'm talking about. Blonde. Big boobs. Total slut. The kind of girl who doesn't need a name. It's always the blonde, isn't it? I guess certain things will turn your hair gold. Francie's hair was hell-of-gold.

As for me: my hair was brown like something you looked for and looked for and couldn't find until your mom told you to check under your bed, and then there it was, crumpled in a dusty corner where you couldn't reach it.

I didn't see Francie again for the rest of that day, and honestly, I was glad. There was something about her that had freaked me out. The way she threw everything off balance. The way the rules didn't seem to apply to her—and not just Ms. Tinker's classroom policies, either. There were deeper rules being violated. When Francie had stripped off the whore's raincoat to reveal herself dressed as a total hooker, the room had been completely silent. The way outer space is silent in the movies, with not even so much as a snicker from Shana Miller or Toby Snyder. That just didn't happen. What I am saying is that Francie Knight was working some powerful shit. You have to be careful around a girl like that.

I wouldn't have minded having some of her mojo for myself, though. I had none. When the first day of school was over, I stood at my locker and couldn't move. It's not because the hall was so crowded, even though it was. That wasn't it.

Kids were pushing past me, rushing for the door in shifting clusters, grabbing at each other, yelling, laughing, whatever, and I just stood there. I didn't see anyone I recognized, and I couldn't bring myself to walk away. I couldn't bring myself to be alone. I was standing there, fingers still on my combination lock, and all I could do was twirl the spinner around and around. *Click, click, click.* And then again. I stood there, a stranger, not even looking at the lock, but instead staring at the floor, watching my reflection in shiny tiles yet to be scuffed. *Click, click, click.* I didn't know where to go. I was invisible.

It didn't matter. I'd stood there so long that the hallway was empty; there was no one around to see me one way or the other. I headed for the back door, the one by the girls' locker room, and pushed my way outside, where I stood at an asphalt path at the top of a hill and looked out over the football field. Off in the distance, a group of girls I used to know had set up a blanket and were lying in their T-shirts and shorts, trying to sun themselves even though summer was really over.

September went like that. I drifted along, talking to almost no one, sitting in the back of classrooms hoping to go unnoticed while other girls lazed at their desks with catlike lassitude, soaking up imaginary glory. Instead of taking notes, I wrote my own name over and over in my spiral-bound notebooks, filling up pages, and was always surprised when I looked down at the crammed blue lines. *Valentina Martinez. Valentina Martinez. Valentina Martinez. Valentina Martinez.* Then I would write it again, just to be sure that it was still my name.

I hadn't always been this way, I knew. It hadn't been so long since I'd had friends. I had once been a regular person. But Emily had moved to California to live with her dad after her mom's nervous breakdown, Kathryn had been sent to boarding school, and Sarah and Jaime had both gotten into a school for smart kids on the other side of the county, an hourlong bus ride away. Emily'd emailed me a few times over the summer to tell me about the crappy weather in San Diego, and that was it. Everyone else just kind of forgot about me. It seemed that I was a very forgettable person.

I was barely there at all.

It had happened to other people, too. People who had always existed—people with names, identities, nice shoes— who had just started to disappear once high school had started.

One time, toward the end of September, I was coming out of the bathroom when I saw this guy, Nick Whitney. I'd known him forever; we'd had classes together since kindergarten. We used to call him Nicky. When I came out of the bathroom that day and found myself face-to-face with him, we locked eyes. There was something about his plaintive expression—his raised eyebrows, his heart-shaped mouth barely open—that made me want to talk to him. *Help,* he seemed to be saying. He was about to say something, and so was I, but before either of us could utter a word, he faded from sight right in front of me. "Nick," I said. "Nicky?" But he was gone. I kept on walking. There was nothing else to do. This was just how it was now.

Weeks went by, and I had almost forgotten about Francie. I mean, you could never totally forget about her: there she was every day in Ms. Tinker's class, or at least three days out of five, and no one could possibly miss the sight of her cutting a wide swath down the halls of Sandra Dee Senior High School in skirts shorter than her high heels, with no books, no backpack, no nothing except her tiny purse and those long, long legs. There was no ignoring Francie, that's the truth. But once I got used to her—once I stopped feeling my shoulders fall every time she walked by—she didn't seem real anymore. She was like a deer you see darting across the road when you're driving along late at night, half asleep in the back of your parents' car. Something startling—unsettling, even—but mostly of another world entirely.

I think everyone felt that way about her. Because although I heard people gossiping about Francie, I never saw a single person actually speak to her. She was supposedly such a slut—according to conversations I'd overheard in Modern Living class—but it was hard to see how she had the chance to hook up with anyone. She was always alone.

Francie hanging outside the girls' room. Francie slinking into Physics late, still with no books. Waiting on the corner before climbing into a strange car. Burning through one thousand Misty Ultra Lights.

She was that kind of girl. She was the kind of girl it was probably better not to think about too much.

September seemed like it went on forever, and then it was over, and I looked back on it and realized that I couldn't remember any of it at all. It was October, and I wondered if the rest of my life was going to be like this. A lonely and indistinct accumulation of pointless days.

I felt like I was losing parts of myself. Just small parts for now; things that you wouldn't notice to look at me. But what if when the leaves on the trees started falling, more important things went missing? What if I woke up one morning to find myself without a big toe or a canine tooth?

One day, it almost happened. I was slinking across the football field toward the park and noticed a breeze that smelled like something burning when I saw the first leaf of autumn. I had picked up the habit of training my eyes on nothing when I walked, just staring off at some unfixed point in the distance, which meant that I sometimes saw things that any other person would miss. Things like a yellowy leaf dislodging from a branch and floating in and out— one plane of focus to the next—until finally landing at the feet of a girl sitting alone in a canyon of concrete bleachers and puffing on a long, skinny cigarette.

It was Francie Knight. A clear afternoon, early autumn, her crazy blond hair curling into white smoke and hovering in the air like messy tendrils of a scattering cloud. There she was, staring into space with a satisfied smirk, looking perfectly happy to be by herself, when the leaf delivered itself to her.

Francie leaned over, picked up the leaf, and looked at it; she twirled it by its stem between her index finger and thumb and let it go. And instead of falling to the ground, the leaf was airborne again, and I swear to God that Francie was looking straight at me—I mean, looking me right in the eye— as it gained altitude, climbing, climbing, and then was gone.

If I didn't know better, I'd have thought that Francie Knight had reversed gravity. She was the kind of girl who might actually be able to do something like that.

Chapter Two

Around here, no one has any parents. There's a long, winding creek that seems to be in everyone's backyard. There's a mall a few miles off, sitting big and solid at the top of a hill, ringed by parking garages. These are the things you know. This is the suburbs.

Around here, there are no sidewalks. In spring azaleas spill out into the street. The parents that people do have definitely don't count. In afternoons, after school, you wander up and down the block, pondering an intention. The mall hangs in the distance, above the trees, blue and indistinct like a mountain range. Most days, you head there. Where else is there to go?

I went to the mall a lot.

It wasn't that I liked shopping all that much. And I

never had any money, anyway, so it basically wouldn't have mattered even if I had wanted to buy something. But there wasn't much else to do, and hanging around the house with my mom was just way too depressing to handle. I had to go somewhere. At the mall, I could pretend that I was someone other than myself.

At the mall, there was something about the bubbling fountains in the atrium that implied a promise. Even if you weren't going to get your wish, at least you could dig through the coins at the bottom and collect a couple of dollars for an Orange Julius.

At the mall, in the beginning of October, there was this whiff of something: like newness, or the future. Or maybe I was just mistaking the smell of Cinnabons and makeup. Either way, walking into any store, I could see myself in a different sweater, a different pair of underwear, and feel like it would really change everything. Like the mall could transform me.

The first time Francie Knight ever said my name, I was at Wet Seal, next to the Guess? store, near Bloomingdale's, pretending I was the kind of person who shopped at Wet Seal. Francie had snuck up behind me.

"Valentina, right?"

And when I turned, she was standing there. In a plain white T-shirt ripped at the collarbone, a white cotton miniskirt over white, cropped leggings, and bright red heels, her hair swept back into a tangled ponytail revealing giant gold hoop earrings that glinted with a hint of something I couldn't put my finger on. She had her small baguette-shaped purse clutched at her hip like a pistol.

And I want to tell you something. You can feel free not to believe me, because it's the kind of thing I'd call bullshit on, too, if I hadn't experienced it myself. But the instant everything changes, you know. It's just like—one second you are one thing, and then you're something else. You feel it like a warm shiver that zings up the backs of your arms, and up and out through the top of your spine, all in one quick rush. A moment of clarity in which, briefly, the entire future of everything is laid out clearly before you and then is gone. A near-life experience. One moment . . . and then.

"Valentina, right?" And zing. Francie Knight had said my name aloud. Everything was different now. There it was.

I wasn't expecting any of it. Yeah, we had one class together. And yeah, there had been that weirdness with the leaf. But just the same, I would never have guessed that Francie would know who I was, much less that she would care. First off, she didn't come to class very often. And second, like I said, no one ever tended to notice me at all. But there she was, right behind me.

"Hey," I said. I didn't move my hand from the rack of clothes I'd been looking at, just cocked my head to the side. I wasn't sure how I was supposed to react.

Francie had already turned away, so my reaction didn't matter. She had moved on to the sale rack, where she was shaking her hips to the beat of the piped-in ABBA on the Muzak, mouthing along to the missing words and flipping through long, sparkly dresses, making exaggerated faces of disapproval at each one. Had she really talked to me, or had I imagined it?

Without looking up, she spoke again. "I don't know about this store," she said. "A little conservative, don't you think? And what about these prices? It's, like, a crime."

"I was just looking," I said.

"Hey, I'm not gonna stop you from shopping at Wet Seal if that's your thing. Everyone has rights. You're in Ms. Tinker's third period, right?"

"Yeah," I said.

Francie finally took her eyes off the clothes on the sale rack and looked up at me. She gave an exaggerated shudder. "What a bitch. One month into school and she's already trying to dock me credit." Francie tucked a lock of hair behind her ear. "Apparently I have too many tardies. My mom writes me notes for the unexcused absences; it's the tardies that are the problem. They don't take notes for those. It's re-tardied."

She raised her eyebrows at her own joke, and plucked something off the rack. It was a red satin halter dress. Kind of ugly and kind of beautiful at the same time. It was hard to decide. Probably more on the ugly side, but you could never be sure until you tried it on. Francie held it up to my chest, pondering.

"Hey, that could actually work," she said. "I really think it could work on you. It's all about proportions." Then, out of nowhere: "Wanna have a cig?"

I'd never smoked a cigarette before and was actually sort of scared at the idea. But it seemed like a bad move to say no to this person who was obviously insane and liable to do just about anything. Plus, I was intrigued. I nodded. Without acknowledgment, Francie just turned and left.

I stood there for a second, confused, and then followed.

I followed Francie out of the store, through the mall, down the tacky, fake marble boulevard. Fountains, potted palms, the light perfectly uniform and yellow, originating from somewhere unknowable. Francie walked quickly. She didn't wait for me. It seemed possible that she had forgotten about me, but I didn't turn back. Every time I thought I'd lost her, I'd see a blur of blond out of the corner of my eye, and there she'd be again, heading in an unexpected direction.

Francie was speeding along with eccentric purpose, as if her cigarette was the last important thing left in the world. She didn't seem to have a clear idea of where she was headed. She just wound her way around corners, up and down escalators, doubling and tripling back on herself in a mystifying spiral. I finally caught up with her in a strange, narrow corridor I'd never noticed, next to Sears, where she spun around with an impish grin, and beckoned with an index finger.

I nodded, barely even realizing I was doing it, and Francie turned around again and ran to the end of the hallway. Without slowing down, she reached out and pushed through a heavy metal door marked EMERGENCY EXIT. I was half a step behind her. I waited for the alarm to sound, but it didn't.

There was a coolness. We had emerged in the parking garage. I guess it was a part of the garage that no one knew about, because it was almost totally empty. An orange pylon in the corner was marked Q-2. I thought the sections only went up to F, but whatever.

Francie stretched her fingers to the concrete ceiling and bounced on the toes of her absurd heels. The only car in sight was a lonely white Ford Thunderbird, parked at an angle between two spaces. "That was a close one," Francie said.

She hopped up onto the hood of the car, reached into her handbag, and pulled out two cigs. She handed one to me and lit her own with a hot-pink Bic.

"Close one?" I slid next to her on the car's hood.

"Just kidding," Francie said. "I never get caught. But still, it's fun to pretend sometimes. It makes things more exciting. I love danger."

She dragged deeply and jerked her head in the direction of my bag. "Well? Check your purse," she said.

I tucked the still unlit Misty into my mouth and reached into the bag and groped around until I found something balled up at the bottom. I pulled it out: the Wet Seal halter dress. Red, shining, and brand-new, with the tags still dangling from a seam at the neck. A dress I hadn't bought. A dress I had not put in my bag.

"How . . . ?"

Francie shrugged and flipped her ponytail, narrowed her eyes, like to say, *No big deal.* "The dress isn't my style," she said. "But I think it'll look good on you. You've got the right look." She leaned over, touched a hand to my hip, and lit my cigarette. "It's all about proportions." A lock of her hair brushed my shoulder. "Pull," she said. She could tell I didn't know what I was doing.

There was a spark and a flicker, and I felt a strange buzz in my chest. I didn't cough. In fact, the smoke filling my lungs felt familiar. It felt like I had been living this way my whole life.

"Let's go to my place," Francie said.

"Sure," I said.

We rode the bus to Francie's house, a big and gorgeous but dog-eared Victorian in a valley on Maple between Poplar and Elm. I don't know where I had expected Francie to live, but it wasn't in a place like the one we strolled up to. Francie's house was pale pink with an elaborately latticed front porch and a white picket fence from which the front gate had come unhinged. It was damp and overcast outside, warm, and the pink of the house was exaggerated cartoonishly against the brownish sky. An old black Jaguar sat in the driveway.

It turned out that Francie didn't live too far away from me—it was walking distance, even—but stepping through her front door, I suddenly felt a million miles away from where I'd started the afternoon. I felt miles from myself.

Inside, Francie's mom was sitting on the couch in the living room, a glass of red wine in her left hand. She had waist-length silver hair, and she was wearing a pair of ratty jeans with a lavender spaghetti-strap tank top. I noticed a faded stain on the front, right between her boobs, which were, by the way, excellent for mom-boobs. Francie's mom didn't seem to be doing much of anything; she was just sitting there with some weird old-timey music on the stereo, swaying along but not quite on the beat. She was kind of beautiful.

"Francie!" Francie's mom said, brightening when she saw us. "How was the mall?"

"Hey, Sandy. The mall was good," Francie said. She turned to me and muttered, "Don't humor her."

"Sit and chat," said Sandy. Francie didn't reply, just bounded up the stairs, beckoning. I gave Sandy an awkward half-wave, then followed Francie before her mother snared me in conversation.

"She's one of those moms who's always talking about how we're supposedly 'best friends,'" Francie said after she had slammed the door to her room and collapsed on her bed. "Her and me, I mean. What the fuck she is talking about, I do not know. And what kind of a person is best friends with her own mother? A total loser, I'm pretty sure. Even if you like your mother, which, P.S., I don't."

I didn't point out that, from what I had seen at school, Francie was in no position to be rejecting applications for best friend. Still, I could see what she was saying.

"Sit," Francie commanded. She patted a spot next to her on the bed, and I sat. She lit another cigarette. "You like New Order?" Francie picked up a remote control and pointed it at the stereo, and there was the spare, blippy syncopation of a synth. Then strings. Then guitar. "No one respects this eighties stuff," she said. "I love the eighties. I wish I had been alive." It didn't surprise me; in fact, I wondered if the reason she was such a freak was because she had transferred to Sandra Dee straight from 1988.

I racked my brain, trying to think of something to say. That was what you were supposed to do when you had a friend, right? Talk? It had been such a long time that I was out of practice. I couldn't think of a single topic of conversation.

"I love your wallpaper," I finally said, and smiled weakly. I immediately felt like an idiot. Francie's wallpaper was fussy and floral like a grandma's guest room. It was kind of hideous. She giggled. Instead of answering, she looked at me with narrowed eyes and a charitable grimace.

"A blonde and a brunette jump off a building," Francie said. I was starting to see that her favorite conversational tactic was to completely switch directions without warning. "Who lands first?"

"Who?" I asked.

"The brunette," Francie said. "The blonde had to stop and ask for directions."

It was the oldest joke; I'd heard it a billion times before. But I laughed anyway, without knowing exactly why. It wasn't just to be polite, but it definitely wasn't because it was funny, either. Maybe it was because I could sense that the punch line was not exactly where it appeared.

"It wasn't a joke," Francie said.

I stopped laughing. So maybe I was wrong.

"Just kidding," Francie said. "Of course it was a joke. I was just trying to prove a point."

There was a certain sizzle in the room, a certain energy that Francie was throwing off. I got the feeling that if it hadn't been for the thumping music, I would have been able to pull my finger through the air and hear a crackle. And I had a feeling that what I said next might change my life: say the right thing, and the road forks one way. Say the wrong thing, and . . .

She tossed me a cigarette, and I lit up, this time without help.

"A blonde and a brunette are driving down the highway," I said. "The brunette is totally speeding, so she asks the blonde to look and see if there's a cop car behind her. So the blonde looks, and says, 'Yeah, there's a cop car.' So the brunette asks her if it has its lights on and the blonde goes, 'Yes, no, yes, no, yes.'"

Francie laughed. "Okay, see, *that* was a joke," she said. "The best part is that it's the brunette who's too stupid to look in her own fucking rearview mirror." She laughed again. "What a dumb slut."

I couldn't tell if she was messing with me or not, but I decided I barely cared. At least someone was paying attention.

"You must think I'm totally weird," Francie said. She flopped onto a pillow and exhaled a giant cloud of smoke. The way she said it implied that she didn't care; I could go ahead and think she was weird. It was fine with her.

"No," I said. "It's just . . . I don't know. I'm not used to making friends this way." I was still sitting on the edge of the bed, back straight. I kept adjusting, trying to find the most natural way to hold the cigarette. It was hard to find something that worked for more than a few seconds.

"You don't have any friends," Francie said. She didn't say it in a mean way, just offhand, like a boring fact, like there are fifty states in the Union. She had been paying more attention in Ms. Tinker's class than I realized. "Don't worry. Neither do I. It's because I'm choosy. I don't just pick up stray girls at the mall all the time, right? Like just walk up and talk to people minding their own business? But there's something about you. I can usually tell."

"Something like what?"

"You're different. You've got, like, that sneaky thing about you."

"A sneaky thing?" No one had ever described me that way before. I was actually kind of flattered.

"Yeah, just sneaky," she told me. "You look like you could get away with some serious shit. For one thing, you're tiny. Like, how tall are you?"

"Five feet," I said. I didn't see where she was going.

"Exactly," she said. "The type of person that people overlook. You'd be out the door before anyone noticed you. I bet you have a dark past, right?"

I shrugged. Francie shifted positions; now she was lying on her belly, chin propped up on her closed fists.

She pushed further: "Lots of secrets? Just admit it; I don't care. Dark secrets—yes or no?"

I couldn't decide whether or not to lie. I couldn't quite decide on the truth, for that matter. This whole afternoon had felt like a test. "Maybe," I finally said.

"Maybe means yes," Francie said. "I knew it."

I stubbed out the cigarette, which was giving me a gaping feeling in the pit of my stomach. "I guess I'll try on the dress," I said.

Outside the window it was dark. But Francie had scarves thrown over all the lampshades, and the room was warm and pinkish and filling quickly with the smoke that spiraled out from between her fingers. New Order was still pushing through the speakers, *thump-thump-buzz* and every now and then a giant thrum that shook me in the gut. Without thinking, I pulled my sweatshirt over my head, and then the dress over my jeans. I shucked off the pants and let them fall around my ankles before stepping back into my shoes and tying the halter around my neck, standing there, in a new, stolen dress, in front of a girl I'd never spoken to before today.

The dress itched a little. I suddenly felt awkward. For one thing, it looked really stupid with sneakers. But more than that, I guess it was because of what I wanted: I wanted to be beautiful. I wanted to be like Francie, and I knew that I never, ever could. Standing there, in front of someone so different from me, in that ridiculous dress, I was revealing all of my stupidest ambitions.

But Francie was looking up at me from the bed with a dazzled smile.

"You should see yourself," she said. "I mean, you should really see yourself. You look like a different person. You look amazing."

And then I did see myself, like from far away, like from an airplane at night, and she was right. Somewhere in the glittering grid of the suburbs, I was there, in Francie's bedroom, and I was glowing through it all. The brightest light. I was beautiful. Anyone could have seen it.

Chapter Three

"So you're going to steal something today, right?" Francie was asking. We were sitting on the J-12 bus, in the back row, on our way to the mall. "I mean, have you given it any more thought?" she asked.

"I don't know," I told her. I looked down at my lap. I flexed my fingers, examining my raggedy nails. Francie's nails were an inch long, bright red, with little foil rainbows glued on. I needed her to do mine next.

"We've been over this," she said. I could hear her fighting to keep the exasperation out of her voice.

"Yeah," I said. "But I'm still not sure." I closed my eyes. "Can't I just go along with you?"

I concentrated hard on the green blobs floating on the backs of my eyelids. I was trying to memorize the bus route, just from the lurches and bounces, the stops and starts. Francie and I had taken the J-12 together exactly four times now, but somewhere between Monday and Thursday this route had become a familiar bass line in my rib cage. Taking slow, steady breaths, I covered my face, visualizing the landmarks outside as we passed each one. Here was the high school, the Burger King, the 7-Eleven where two girls had killed themselves. We were on the edge of the suburbs, on the seedy stretch of outlying highway where the sky was always the exact same shade of gray and fast-food restaurants were clustered drive-thru to drive-thru. We were almost at the mall.

"Listen, I'm not going to force you or anything," Francie said. "All I'm saying is there's nothing wrong with it, you know? It's just shoplifting. It's not like *abortion.*" She laughed wickedly.

I opened my eyes, startled. I had practically forgotten she was there. "It's not that I think there's anything wrong with it," I said. "And, like, I would care if there was?"

Francie gave me a *don't bullshit me* kind of look. She put a hand on my knee. "Val. It's just taking back what belongs to us already. I mean, it's getting what we deserve. You have to remember that. It's our right. Because don't we deserve more than this?" She fluttered her hand in the air to indicate not just the bus we were sitting on, but every crappy thing in the world.

"Obviously," I said.

The thing is, Francie had gotten it all twisted. She thought I had some kind of moral problem with shoplifting. Well, anyone except a lunatic like her can see that it's technically wrong. But stealing some dumb ten-dollar earrings from Cinderella Club didn't bother me very much. It wasn't that.

"I'm just saying," Francie said. She was working herself up as she talked, becoming more and more rapturous in her conviction. "It's not just our right, okay? It's, like, our duty. It's, like, if we don't do it, who else is going to? Someone has to change things. Take a stand and all that. Think Robin Hood."

Francie was gripping my shoulders with each hand; she had a crazed glint in her eyes.

I nodded seriously, trying to convince her that I got the message. "I know," I said. "You're legitimately right."

Francie looked like she was going to keep going, but the bus pulled to a stop and the hydraulic doors opened with a wheeze. We had arrived. We stood together and climbed down onto the sidewalk.

Standing there outside the mall in the predusk October light, Francie looked like someone out of a myth—probably something Norse, I'd say, because they're the tallest and most imposing. Not to mention blond. She put a hand on my hip. She was glowing, rosy and optimistic in the end of the daylight.

She turned to me and said, "Okay, here's the thing, Val. I'm going to put it a different way and then I'll shut up, I promise. I believe the world is pretty fucking generous. It's just putting all this stuff out there, all laid out in front of us, just free to take. Wouldn't it be stupid not to grab it? It would be irresponsible. What's that thing they say about a horse with a bow on it? Whatever. I'm just telling you what I believe. You don't have to agree or anything. I'm just saying."

Francie believed a lot of things, I was beginning to realize. Some of them seemed pretty retarded. But at least it was nice to be friends with someone who put so much thought into everything. Even when I'd had friends, it never seemed like they cared about much beyond which pages had been assigned in Algebra and who was invited to what birthday party.

Francie and I stood together, our hair twisting behind us in the wind, looking up at the mall. From the outside, it was a fortress, sitting on top of a giant hill off Georgia Avenue and protected by concrete moats of seemingly impenetrable parking garages. To get inside by car was no problem—you just drove on in—but on foot it felt sneaky from the start. You had to slip through fissures that weren't meant for people. That day Francie and I climbed off the J-12 and looked up at Montgomery Shoppingtowne hovering above us, and I felt a funny combination of awe and dread. It was us against this. This sleeping, hungry thing.

Of course, Francie had a plan of attack.

"Over here," she said. She led me from the sidewalk to a chain-link fence that bordered the steep, grassy hill leading up to the first garage. "This way's quickest," she said, and she pointed to a spot where the fence had buckled in on itself and was sagging into the dirt. Francie scrambled over the fence and bounded up the hill, those five-inch heels sinking into the soggy grass as she miraculously managed to keep her balance in them. "Come on," she half shouted. "It's not like it's a crime or anything, but it's probably better if no one sees you. It's just the easiest way."

"Can't we just use the actual door?" I asked.

"You gotta start thinking different," Francie said. "We strike silently. In and out. This way they'll never see us coming."

In Physics, Ms. Tinker had taught us that, in order for the equations to work, you first had to accept certain things. Things that were just for the sake of argument. Things like, for the purposes of this equation, there is no such thing as friction. Or if you drop a rubber ball to the ground a million times, and every time it falls and then bounces back into the air, there's still no guarantee that the same thing will happen on the million-and-first time. For all anyone knew, the ball could turn into a canary and fly away. You had to learn to live with things like that, or there was no point even bothering with physics in the first place. Francie was the same. In order to understand her—I mean, really get what she was saying—you had to first accept, as premise, things that made absolutely no sense.

So I followed her, and we made our way up the hill, hunched and practically crawling to keep from sliding all the way back down. At the top Francie hiked her skirt up, revealing floral biker shorts underneath, and climbed up onto a concrete overhang from which she leaped straight into the parking structure. She gave her hips a little shake, and I climbed right behind her. This is how we made our way into the mall.

And on that overhang I looked over my shoulder, down the hill to the highway, where I saw the bus that had dropped us off crawling into the distance. Just by standing there I was different, I knew. It was way too late to change my mind.

I had always been good. I had always done everything right—done it just how I was supposed to. I had always shown up on time, gone through the motions. My grades had always been decent, but not outstanding enough to be obnoxious. I had never, ever bothered anyone. Because it seems like what most people in the world want is for you to just make yourself as inconspicuous as possible. That was *good*.

Standing there on the outside of the parking garage, though, I was starting to wonder if there wasn't that much difference between being good and being scared.

Because that was just it, obviously: I was scared to steal.

Not scared of getting caught—not scared of going to jail, or hell, or anything like that. What scared me was the thought of that moment. The split second when it stopped belonging to someone else and belonged to me. When I stopped being good and started taking what Francie believed I deserved. What if it turned out I didn't deserve it at all?

That day in the mall, Francie and I sat on the bench outside the Limited, on the ground floor. Francie reached into her purse and pulled out two carefully folded Bloomingdale's bags. She handed one to me, and unfolded the other one as she talked. "There are three and only three tools for shoplifting," Francie instructed me. "Number one: a shopping bag. From an expensive store is best. Ideally you fill it halfway with something like balled-up newspaper to make it look like you've actually been shopping. Number two: a rubber band. Keep it wrapped around your wrist and a few extras in your pocket." She nodded at me as she spoke to make sure I was getting it all. "Number three is liquid eyeliner. Applied heavily and frequently. That's all you need."

"That's it?" I asked.

"That's it," Francie said. "Some people like to carry a can opener, or wear, like, one of those big puffy coats, but I'm not into that. The can opener's overkill, and the puffy coat makes you look like an idiot."

Why? I could have asked. *Why a rubber band? What's the reason?* But I didn't bother. Maybe it had to do with

Francie's eyes, which were green with rings of gold around the pupils, eyeliner stretching to curly points halfway up her temples. Francie's eyes made it hard to concentrate. Or. Not the eyes, I guess, but the liner. Liquid. Applied heavily and frequently.

"Thanks for showing me all that," I said. "It's nice of you to let me in on your secrets."

"*Nice*," Francie said scornfully, half laughing. "Nice. Ugh! Nice is the last thing I'm trying to be. What a bitchy thing to say!" She smiled to show she wasn't quite serious, but it still stung.

"I wasn't trying to be bitchy," I said.

"Argh! That's just it! Like there's something wrong with being bitchy!" Francie pulled her fingers through the roots of her hair, clutching at her scalp. Now she was frustrated. "See, there's your problem right there."

"Um, sorry?" I said.

"Let me ask you a question," Francie said. She looked at me sternly with eyes that appeared to hover a couple inches in front of the rest of her face. "Let me ask you a question: Every day I see you in Ms. Tinker's class—"

"You never come to Ms. Tinker's class," I interjected.

"Well, when I do," Francie said. "Whatever. You know what I mean. Every day you're in your seat when the bell rings, with your pen out and your notebook open. And every day I see you hand your homework up, same as everyone else, and all perfect handwriting and everything. And what I want to know is, why bother? Why do any of it? What's the payoff here, Val? A college recommendation, like, someday? Do any of your teachers even remember you after the bell rings?"

"Ms. Tinker thinks my name is Vickie," I admitted. "I never bothered correcting her, and now it's too late to say anything. Also, she deducts five points if I don't write in cursive, and another five if I forget to put the date on it, and one point for every doodle in the margin. Oh, and two if any of the binder holes are ripped."

"Exactly," said Francie. "What a complete asshole. Have you ever even once thought about just saying fuck it?"

"Yeah," I said.

"Well, why don't you? Why don't you just stop bothering once and for all?"

"I don't know," I said.

Of course, I did know. I was scared. I was scared of lots of things—say, all of the above—but what I was most scared of was Francie. What I was most afraid of was that she would find out exactly what a pussy I really was. From the first time we'd met, I felt like she had the wrong idea about me. She'd said there was something about me, but I suspected she'd seriously misjudged.

I was not sneaky. All my dark secrets technically belonged to other people. And I had always been good. Why, I don't know. Good was just something that came naturally. Maybe it all had to do with my brother, who had always, always been the opposite. Now he was dying. Being good might not be very exciting, but at least you don't die.

"Come on," Francie said. "It's all cool. Let's go." She stood, and snapped the bracelet of rubber bands against her wrist, wincing to herself.

I stood, too. "Next stop Nordstrom," she said. "Watch what I do. You might learn something."

We made our way through the mall to the department store. "I'm not going to let anything hurt you," Francie told me as we walked. "You know that, right?"

She had surprised me. "What?" I asked.

"You have this thing about you. It would be a shame for anything bad to happen to you. I'm not trying to get you in any trouble. Trust me, as long as you're with me, I'll keep you safe. Swear to God."

"Okay," I said. Then, without thinking about it, I leaned over and kissed her on the cheek. I just had to. No one had ever said something like that to me before.

That day, like every day, Nordstrom was echoing with the tinkling, clumsy strains of Pachelbel's Canon on a grand piano, as played by an idiot in a tuxedo in an alcove by the escalator. Francie marched on, through Intimate Apparel to Cosmetics and straight to the Dior counter, where a prissy, overplucked guy in a skintight T-shirt was eyeing us suspiciously from behind the register.

"Hi, girls," he said. "Can I help you with something?"

"I need some makeup," Francie said. "I want the good stuff."

"All our products are good," he said.

"Yeah, I'm sure," Francie said. "This is a store, right? You sell things?"

The clerk gave a deep, pained sigh and started pulling stuff for her like it was the last thing in the world he wanted to do.

Francie winked at me when he wasn't looking and when he'd laid a smorgasbord of makeup in front of her, she began to deliberate, hemming and hawing over all of it, trying on everything he offered her and finding some petty problem with each item. "This black's a little too black," she said. "Do you have anything with a little more blue in it?" And the guy would sigh again and pull out something else.

I kept my eyes glued to her, like she'd told me. I knew exactly what she was doing, but as closely as I watched, I didn't see her take anything. She was just that good.

Watching her, seeing the casual, easy way she had, I wanted more than anything to be like that. Francie was not afraid of anything. She truly did not give a shit. I wanted to be like her. I wanted to be the type of person who believed in something, even if it was something crazy and sort of ridiculous. I wanted to be beautiful, but not beautiful like one of those girls in perfume ads. I wanted to be beautiful like Francie. She was burning, brilliant with courage and self-assurance. There was something about her that was not *good* but really kind of perfect.

As she had promised, it was all there, right in front of me, just asking to be taken. Wouldn't it be careless of me—irresponsible, even—not to take advantage?

So I did it. It was easier than I'd thought it would be. It was just like doing anything else, like buttoning your shirt or opening a book. I reached across the counter and grabbed a tube of liquid eyeliner from its display by the register. It was that simple. It belonged to the mall, and then it belonged to me. Just like that. It was that simple, but I kept it cupped in the palm of my hand, ready to drop it if I needed to.

Francie and the salesguy, whose name turned out to be Clint, were deep in debate about the importance of lip liner, with Francie taking the affirmative position. Clint was more circumspect. "Sometimes it can look a little cheap, if you're not careful or if the contrast is too intense," he was saying, to Francie's emphatic head-shaking. Neither of them had noticed what I had just done.

I waited for her, heart pounding, breathing shallow, imagining beads of sweat forming on my upper lip. Francie was taking her time. She and Clint had gone from being adversaries to BFFs, and they were joking around about Paris Hilton's wonky eye. I couldn't take it anymore.

"Hey, Francie?" I said. She looked up like she'd forgotten all about me.

"Yeah, babe?"

"I really have to pee," I said.

"Oh," said Francie. "Okay, let's go." She turned back to Clint, who was pissed off again. "I don't think any of this works," she said. "I'll come back another time, okay?"

"Fine," he muttered, gathering everything up. Francie and I left the store.

I was still nervous. But there was something about having Francie next to me—her boundless confidence a halo that enveloped both of us. It was her hair. Her eyeliner. The sunny warmth of her undivided, overpowering attention. She was my friend. As long as I was with her, I didn't have anything to worry about. We walked through the exit together, in lockstep, leaving the cameras, the security guards, the smarmy clerks, all of it, just leaving it all behind. There was a shrill beep from above us as we stepped through the antitheft sensors, and Francie whispered, "Just keep on walking." And I did. No one tried to stop us.

"I got something for you," she said when we were safe in the atrium, the smell of Francie's Thierry Mugler Angel mixing with the chlorine from the fountain. "I know you thought I was ignoring you, but it was all part of the plan." She reached into her bag and pulled it out: a new tube of Dior eyeliner, liquid. She presented it with a grin. "The best presents are always stolen," she said.

"Thanks," I said. I waved her off, trying to look casual.

"But I already have my own." Francie looked surprised. I tossed my hair, trying to copy the way she always did it, and with a careless flick of my wrist revealed my own tube, still in the palm of my hand.

She squealed. "Oh my God," she exclaimed breathlessly, and she threw herself on me, wrapped her arms around my neck and a leg around my waist. "You did it! You totally did it."

I stood stick straight, kind of embarrassed because we were making a real spectacle, right there in the middle of the mall. But I had to smile. Francie was squealing and hugging me and jumping up and down.

"Francie!" I finally said. She was making me tense. "Please!" She laughed and pulled away.

"I'm just so proud of you," she said. "Go ahead, put it on. Oh my God! You're going to look great. Dior's the best, best, best—I mean, real top-of-the-line shit, the finest there is." She handed me her compact to use as a mirror. "They never give you enough in the bottle, though. Cheap fucking assholes." Francie sighed as an afterthought.

I unscrewed the tube, looked at the foam-tipped brush, and then thought better of it.

"You do it," I said. "You're the expert."

Francie was gratified. "Sit," she said. And I perched on the edge of the fountain and closed my eyes. I concentrated on the green blobs again, and imagined Francie's lips, bright red, lined with eggplant, and twisted into deep, satisfied concentration. I imagined each tiny movement of her hands as I felt the cold brush across my face. Francie's bangles were barely jangling in my ear, and I pictured sparks flying. I could have sat like that forever, or at least a really long time. But Francie was well practiced. It only took her a minute.

"Okay, open up," she said. I opened my eyes to the sight of Francie, radiant with openness and generosity. "You look so badass," she said. "Babe, you are legitimately the baddest." She held up the mirror, but I didn't need to look. I already knew what I had become.

Around here, very small things can transform you. There's a winding creek that seems to touch every backyard. You put a toe in the freezing water and shudder, but a good kind of shudder because you're happy just to feel anything at all.

On days when you have nothing better to do, you go to the mall. You are hoping to be a better person. Or a worse one. You ask the mall for what you want. And if you want it enough, you'll get it. Because it's all laid out right there in front of you. It would be stupid—irresponsible, even—not to take what's being offered.

Chapter Four

At school, no one noticed that I was different. It was easy for them not to notice because they still didn't notice me at all. I was the same as ever. I was no one.

I still sat in the back row, hair hanging in my face, drawing listless curlicues in my notebook while some teacher droned on. I still showed up for class on time, handed in enough homework to pull B-pluses, and walked through the halls with my shoulder grazing the lockers, books flat at my chest. I didn't look any different. Well, except for the eyeliner. And I didn't really act any different, either.

But I was different. No one had any idea how much I had changed. I liked it that way. I was fooling them all.

A few days before Halloween, I was headed to Physics when Francie beckoned to me from a door by the cafeteria that I'd never noticed before. She was standing in the doorway, hip cocked, forearm resting against the jamb. "C'mere," she hissed, waving frantically. "I need to show you something."

"I have Physics," I said. "And so do you, come to think of it."

"Oh, for fuck's sake," Francie said. "I'm not going to argue with you! Come *on*."

I wavered for a split second, but let's be real: of course I went with her. Everyone else skipped class all the time; I figured I could do it once without Ms. Tinker even noticing. And Francie had, like, this power over me. So I stepped through the door and followed her into a musty, dark stairwell.

"I can't believe I found this," Francie said. She lit a cigarette and handed me one.

"No thanks," I said.

"I thought it was just going to be a broom closet or something, but false! It turns out to be, like, some kind of secret passage! Truly insane."

"I swear to God I never saw that door before," I said.

"Really? That's weird. Sometimes you have to be looking, I guess." She was standing only inches away from me, and I could feel the heat from her cherry on my face. It lit her up, all orange and spooky in the dark of the barely illuminated stairwell.

"Come on," Francie said.

We walked down mildewy concrete stairs, deep into the bowels of the school, me trailing my fingers along the cinder block walls the whole way. I read somewhere that you can find your way out of any maze by keeping a hand pressed against the wall as you walk. Even though our path was a straight line, I thought it was better to be on the safe side. Then, finally, the stairs ended, and we continued on, down a narrow, subterranean corridor, our way lit only by weak, caged-in sconces on the walls. Francie bounced ahead of me, totally unworried about the possibility that we were most likely heading straight into the lair of a serial killer or, at best, the pervy janitor.

I tried to figure out exactly where we were relative to the rest of the school—tried to imagine what was going on above our heads—but it was too confusing. I couldn't orient myself. We were just getting more and more removed from everything real. And then Francie stopped, waiting for me, and when I caught up, I saw that we'd come to a dead end—the passageway ended in a steel ladder bolted to the wall, which led to a trapdoor in the ceiling.

Francie gave a deep curtsy. "My most awesome discovery ever," she crowed.

"Where does it go?" I asked.

"Just see!" she said.

"You go first," I told her.

"Ha," she said. "Trust me—it's not scary. But fine." And

she scrambled up the ladder, undid the latch in the trap-door, and disappeared above me. I took a deep breath and followed.

I poked my head out on the other side, into what seemed to be a tiny supply closet. Francie was perched on a plastic milk crate. She had her high heels dangling from her toes.

"Um, it's a closet," I said, pulling myself out of the trap-door. "Awesome." I didn't see what was so great about a closet.

Francie just winked and opened the door, and light flooded our closet, leaving me momentarily blinded. When my eyes finally adjusted, all I saw was green grass and blue sky. I laughed in surprise. The passage had led us straight out of the school. We were in the supply shed at the far end of the football field.

"No more sneaking past security guards or any of that crap," Francie said. She was making fun of me, sort of, knowing that I had never snuck past a school security guard in my life. "Three steps and we're off school property. Free! Seriously, could anything be better?"

I laughed again. "It's pretty awesome," I said. Francie took my hand, and we left the shed, careful not to let the door latch behind us. We made our way through the trees into the park behind the school, and down past the bike path, to the hidden creek, where we settled in on the pebbly bank. This time I accepted Francie's offer of a cigarette. She sat next to me, puffing thoughtfully, and she gave me a serious look. "So I want to show you something really important," she said. "I've been waiting till I thought you were ready. And I think you're ready now. You did such an awesome job at Nordstrom the other day. It's time."

"Um, okay," I said.

"Okay," said Francie. "First off, you have to promise that you'll never reveal what I'm about to tell you. Promise?"

"Duh," I said. With Francie I'd learned it was often just better to go with the flow and figure things out later. Trying to get a straight explanation out of her before she was ready was usually more trouble than it was worth.

"I promise," I said. Francie reached over and took my hand and squeezed it, looking me straight in the eye.

"Even if they torture you," Francie said. "Like, especially in the face of torture. Promise?"

I couldn't not roll my eyes. "Okay already!" I said.

"Good," she said.

Francie tugged on her left earlobe. She tugged on her right earlobe. She wiggled her nose twice like the lady from *Bewitched*, except it was more of an up-and-down bunny twitch than a witchy back-and-forth.

I stared at her, waiting for her to tell me what she was going to tell me. She didn't say anything.

"Well?" I finally asked. "Don't get me all excited and then kill me with suspense or anything."

Francie tugged on her left earlobe. She tugged on her

right earlobe. She wiggled her nose again. "Got it?" she asked.

"Um, no," I said.

"It's the Sign," she said. "I'm showing you the Sign."

"You mean that stuff you were doing?"

"Yes," Francie said. "Try it."

I tugged on my earlobes, copying her as she did it along with me: left, then right, then wiggled my nose. I felt like a fool.

"You got it," Francie said.

"I got it, but I don't get it," I said.

"What's not to get?"

"What's the point of it?" I asked. "I mean, why are you showing me this?"

"It's, like, if you're ever in trouble," Francie said. "Like, if things get desperate. Like, if you're about to be caught. You make the signal, and hopefully someone will recognize it and help you out."

"Who's going to recognize?" I asked.

"Another member of our sisterhood," she said. "There are more of us than you know, Val. More of us than I know, either. It's, like, all ancient and everything. It goes so far beyond you and me. A sisterhood. It's been around for thousands of years—as long as anyone's been stealing. They used this sign in the open-air markets of ancient Mesopotamia. So now I'm passing it on to you. You're a member of the club."

"Uh-huh," I said.

"No, seriously," Francie said.

It was hard not to look skeptical. "So who, like, told you about it?" I asked.

"I can't reveal," Francie replied, with a mysterious shrug.

Of course, it was all totally idiotic. The Sign itself seemed like something that a five-year-old made up on the playground, and the idea that there was some centuries-old network of shoplifters stretching back to ancient Mesopotamia was even more dumb. If anyone else had told me any of this stuff, I would have laughed out loud.

But this was Francie. A girl who could find doorways where they'd never been before. A girl who had been known to reverse gravity. A girl who could make anything—anything—disappear.

She had proven herself to be a master of the unlikely. Why start doubting her now?

"Got it now?" she asked.

Instead of answering, I tugged at my earlobes and twitched my nose.

"Perfecto," Francie said.

We stood, and as we dusted our butts off, there was a giant gust of wind, and leaves began to fall. We stood there, on the edge of the creek, looking up as red autumn leaves flew around us in an unexpected cyclone.

"Let's go to the mall," Francie said.

"Now?"

"Yeah, we're already out. Why not?"

I thought it over. There were still four periods left in the day; I had a quiz in Geometry.

"Okay," I said. "Let's go."

Chapter Five

"Do you believe in God?" Francie asked one day in her bedroom.

"Yes," I said. "Do you?"

"No," said Francie. "Well, not really. Maybe a little. So do you, like, read the Bible and stuff?"

"No," I said. "But I went to Sunday school when I was little."

"So you know about Samson and Delilah, then."

"Maybe?" I said. "It sounds familiar, but I'm not sure."

"I read the Bible over the summer and it was totally boring," Francie said. "But Samson and Delilah was one good part of it. It's, like, about this superhero named Samson and his bitchy girlfriend, Delilah."

"Oh, wait. Is he the one with the ponytail?" I asked.

"Yes," Francie said. "A long beautiful ponytail, like three feet long, and very shiny. And he had these superpowers, superstrength and whatnot. But then one night when he's asleep, the bitch Delilah sneaks up to him with a pair of, like, shears and chops off all his hair." Francie punctuated herself by scissoring her fingers through the air maniacally, *snip-snip-snip*.

"Why'd she do that?" I asked.

"I forget." Francie shrugged. "The devil probably. Anyway, then the next day he goes on this mission where he has to, like, hold up a temple while it's collapsing. Or something like that; I'm just going on memory. Whatever. Normally it would have been no problem for him because he was just that strong. But it turned out that all his powers were in his hair. Without the ponytail he was just some regular dude. So the temple collapses on him and he dies."

"What a bitch. I hope Delilah was sorry."

"Probably not," Francie said. "They never are. It's a crazy story, though, right? And it teaches such an important lesson."

"What's the lesson?"

"Appearances count," said Francie. "Even in Bible times, it was so important to have good hair."

"He probably looked better without the ponytail," I pointed out.

"Maybe they were more in style in those days," Francie said. "Like in the nineties."

I looked down at myself, at my jeans, not too baggy and

not too tight, and my blue zip-up hoodie. I twirled a limp strand of hair around my finger. I looked over at Francie.

"Cut my hair," I said.

"I really don't think that was the point of the story!" Francie laughed. "Unless you want to be crushed in a tragic collapsing-temple accident."

"I'm sick of it," I said. I thrust forward a lock of my limp brown hair. "It just, like, hangs there."

"Okay," Francie said. "Let's do it, Samson. You could hardly be less superstrong than you already are." She picked a pair of scissors up off her desk and led me to the bathroom, where I sat on the edge of the bathtub. Francie draped a towel over my shoulders. "I've never really cut hair before, but it can't be too hard, right?"

"I'm sure it's easy," I said.

"How do you want it to look?" Francie asked.

"Different," I said.

And Francie took the scissors and just went to town, her tongue poking from her mouth as hair started flying everywhere. I'd been growing it out since elementary school, but I wasn't very sorry to see it go. It was the old me.

"No, don't look!" she yelped when she was done and I made a move to the mirror. "I have to put some *product* in it."

She dumped some sticky crap in her palms, rubbed them together, and then gunked it around on my head. "Okay, now you can look," she said. Around us, the bathroom was completely covered in scraps of dark hair.

Appearances count. The Bible teaches us this. Although I believe in God, I don't put much stock in the Bible; it's just way too long. But appearances do count. Look at poor Samson and that bitch Delilah. A different hairdo and everything would have swung the other way.

The next day, I showed up at school in a tight white shift dress that stopped six inches above my knees and a pair of white go-go boots borrowed from Francie. My hair was gone; now it was just a spiky, dark crown at my skull. It looked great.

Everyone stared at me when I walked into Physics. All heads turned at once. "Slut," I heard Shana Miller cough under her breath. That was Shana Miller for you. Ms. Tinker pushed her glasses up on her nose and regarded me for a brief moment. "Valerie," she said. "You're late. See me after class."

Francie was sitting at her desk already, grinning from ear to ear.

I'd thought it would feel different. To look like this, to dress like this. To be this person. I had thought I would feel powerful. Unstoppable, like Francie. Instead, I was embarrassed. Who did I think I was?

Appearances definitely count, but I also had to wonder if Francie had missed the point of Samson and Delilah. Because, to me, the real question was exactly the question that she had glossed over. The question I asked Francie—the one she blew off—cuts right to the point of everything: Why'd Delilah do it?

Chapter Six

You take a seashell. You take a tube of lip gloss and a prissy silk scarf like an English teacher would wear. You take a mountain, and a cloud, and a molten pebble from the core of the world. Francie said this was how we were going to do it. Because the entire planet Earth is pretty fucking big. You have to start small and take a chunk at a time.

That was Francie's theory, at least.

Francie claimed that she had been shoplifting for at least as long as she could remember, and even though I didn't quite believe her, the thing is that it almost would have made more sense for it to be true. Maybe she had been born with a popped antitheft sensor in one hand and a rubber band in the other. Because when it came to stealing, Francie was amazing, I am telling you. Amazing. Like that first day at the mall, at Wet Seal, when she'd stolen the red dress: one minute it was in her hand and then it was in my purse, in my size and everything. An offering of friendship. All she had to do was want something and it was hers. She had wanted not just the dress but, for whatever reason, me.

Well, Francie wanted everything. By *everything* I mean every single thing. Sometimes it seemed like there was a clandestine line of ascendancy, like Francie knew she was waiting in the wings to rule an oblivious world. Francie had a sparkle in her eye that suggested she had a secret, and the secret was that you couldn't even begin to imagine her destiny. A girl-queen in exile.

"I have a plan," she told me one day in November, a few weeks after she had showed me the Sign. We were standing by the glass elevator on the mezzanine level, looking down over early Christmas shoppers milling around the wide pavilion below us. The glowing signs and kiosks were laid out like a set of instructions to be followed, and Francie leaned out on tiptoe, palms facedown against the guardrail. She turned to me with a mischievous slant of the eyebrow and said, "All this is going to be ours." The tiny silver lima bean around her neck quivered at the hollow of her clavicle. Breath in, breath out. I thought I saw a spark.

Start with a shitty plastic charm bracelet. Have a plan. "Why stop at stupid, tacky Montgomery Shoppingtowne?"

Francie wanted to know. "Between the two of us, we can do it. We clean this place out first, then expand the operation. It already belongs to us, anyway. We just need to claim it." With Francie's voice hoarse from cigarettes, it was always hard to tell how serious she was. Of course, by then I had learned that questions like that were basically immaterial.

"We'll clean this place out," I said, going along with her. "Then move on to the Smithsonian."

So Francie and I went to the mall every day after school. We held our little black bags close to our hips and closer to our fingers, always looking out for that one thing that caught our eye. "It's easy," she explained to me when I asked her for her secrets. "Just pretend you're the sun. Too hot to look at. Anyone looks at you too long—burn 'em. Remember that and you'll never get caught."

It wasn't exactly that easy. There were tools and techniques. There were strategies she taught me—strategies in which I will never lose my expertise. Rubber bands, bottle openers, booster bags, decoys. Angles to be worked out. You had to know the blind spots. But, according to Francie, not one of those specifics was nearly as important as what she called "the becoming."

"The becoming" was what you told yourself before the hit. It was reminding yourself that it all belonged to you, and that you were doing nothing wrong. It was leaving your own body and letting something fearless and hungry inhabit it instead. In Francie's case, it was donning a spooky, blinding camouflage. It was channeling the sun. Too hot to look at. That was just Francie. For me, it turned out, it was something entirely different.

Francie knew that the closer it got to Christmas, the less anyone at the mall had time to worry about a couple of teenage girls. Around the holiday, according to her, you could really go crazy. So we ditched seventh period on Friday afternoon the week before Thanksgiving and caught the bus down Georgia Avenue to the mall.

I still hadn't stolen anything big. Up till then it had been all trinkets for me; junky crap that no one would care about if they caught me. And even when it came to that stuff, I was so unsmooth that I couldn't figure out why Francie thought I would make a suitable accomplice. Just the intention of stealing anything made me edgy: eyes darting, mouth twitching, movements all jerky, totally suspicious-looking. It was a miracle I hadn't been busted.

For some reason, Francie believed in me despite my complete amateurishness. She believed that I had something special and had decided that it was time for me to take it to the next level. To steal big, earn my stripes. Thanksgiving being the perfect time for it. I wasn't sure how I felt about the idea. Okay, I did know how I felt about it. Not good.

"It's all about the *becoming*," she explained for the trillionth time on the bus ride over. "You get that down and you'll be able to steal anything at all. You'll be fine, I promise. I can always tell."

I hadn't really figured out what she was talking about with that business, which sounded kind of New Age-y to me. But I tried to act confident as we marched into the Limited, the two of us with loping, tigery strides, Francie in a pink tulle ballerina skirt and me in a checked micromini jumper.

The confidence was just an act, obviously. I hadn't gotten any more comfortable dressing this way since my haircut. I just kept it up to make Francie happy. To experience the look of unvarnished pride on her face when she saw me in a shorter skirt, a higher pair of heels. She said it gave me *gravity*, and I guess that part was good, because before I'd met Francie, I had been worried that I might just float away.

As soon as we stepped into the store that day, Francie touched my hand, smiled, and made a casual beeline for the sale racks in the back corner, leaving me by myself. We had a plan. Or more like Francie had a plan and I was a part of it. I was just happy to be a player in her grand scheme—a scheme that I imagined to be part of an even grander one, and then another on top of that.

But on that particular day, the agenda was as simple as it was practical. Francie would run distraction in the sale racks while I worked the bigger-ticket items near the entrance. I was going to hit big.

Francie headed to the back, clearing her throat and

rustling clothes as she walked, touching everything she passed, unfolding shirts and knocking them aside, drawing stares from every quarter. Her neckline plunged halfway down her chest, and she had her boobs pushed up around her shoulders, thanks to some mysterious undergarment. How could you not stare? No one was paying any attention to me at all, which really was the whole point.

I wandered the front of the store aimlessly, my eyes swinging back and forth in search of the perfect thing to steal. They were blasting Shakira, but I could still hear Francie from the back of the store as if she was standing right next to me. "Excuse me? Excuse me, ma'am? This shirt has a hole in it. Right here. See? Right there next to the collar. How should I know how it got there? Do you think I could get a discount? I'll give you four ninety-nine."

Francie was chattering away. She had a talent for spectacle. I didn't look in her direction, but even without looking I could see her vamping and showboating, tossing her hair and batting her mascara-greased eyelashes until she had dark, scratchy lines etched above her cheekbones. When she wanted to, Francie had this absolute force of presence. I could have seen her with my eyes closed; I could have seen her with a blindfold on.

Someone had put the jacket away wrong. I'd noticed a rack of black leather motorcycle jackets right by the entrance as soon as I'd stepped into the store, but I hadn't paid much attention, since they were all wired to a central alarm system that would go off if you tried to unplug any of them, and I had nowhere near the nerve for that. But then, passing a lonely column of fleece hoodies, I spied the hint of a leather sleeve peeking out from behind the plush, bright microfiber.

I looked again. It was unmistakable. Peeling back the layers of hoodies, I saw it, there by itself, free for the taking. No sensor, no alarm, no ink tag. A black leather zip-front motorcycle jacket, sleek and slim with a Nehru collar. Someone had put it away wrong. And I can't really tell you if I believe in fate or not, but the fact of the matter is that at that moment it seemed like the jacket had been waiting for me. I wanted it.

I looked at the price tag: $300.50. I looked around. No one was paying attention to me. But I couldn't do it. Just standing that close to it made me feel like I was attracting suspicion.

Be the sun, Francie had said.

It had seemed like good advice at the time, but when it came time to implement it, the total uselessness of it struck me. *Too hot to look at,* I said to myself, and I pictured myself on fire. I pictured myself as a spinning disco ball, throwing flash in every direction; as a bolt of lightning; as a shattering star, a flaming arrow shooting for a bull's-eye. But I wasn't any of those things. I was not the sun. I wasn't even a blonde.

I was myself. Even if I had fooled Francie into thinking I was someone important, it didn't change the fact that I was

Valentina Martinez. People like me didn't steal things, and they definitely didn't wear jackets like this one.

I stared at it. It was gorgeous—more gorgeous on further inspection than it had even first appeared. I toyed with a sleeve, rubbed the cuff between my fingers, feeling the leather. It was soft—too soft. Almost like it was still alive. And when I ran the back of my hand against the jacket's breast pocket, I could feel something like a rhythm beneath the surface of the material, beating back against my knuckles.

Something happened. Off in what sounded like the distance, I could hear Francie squabbling with a clerk. I paid no attention. I couldn't understand what she was saying, and I didn't care. There was something building inside of me, a black inky rage that I couldn't quite understand. It was anger, but not the kind I was used to from my brother and stepfather. This was something quieter; something slithering and austere. It was powerful. Subtle. I liked it.

Then I was putting on the jacket. I just put it on. I'm not saying I was possessed or anything; it wasn't like that. I knew exactly what I was doing. I just took it off the rack, without a thought, and slipped it on and zipped it up, and as the zipper closed, I was surprised to find that it felt like I was shedding a skin instead of gaining a new one. Without hesitation, I turned and walked out of the store, not thinking, *I just stole a three-hundred-dollar jacket,* but thinking, *This jacket looks amazing on me.* Not wondering where Francie was or what she was doing, but knowing without a doubt that she was right on my heels.

Francie and I had decided to meet in the handicap stall by Sears. The handicap bathroom at any mall is always deserted and is generally hidden somewhere in a dim alcove somewhere off the beaten path. There's usually a handicap stall by the food court, too, but Francie and I tried to avoid those because they were always full of bulimics. The "handicap" part was important because the wheelchair stall was big enough for two people, with a door that went all the way to the tiles so no one could tell you were in there. That was where we caught our breath every day before heading home. It was where we took the loot from our bags, unballed it, and held it out at arm's length, admiring it all under spastic white fluorescent light. Where we congratulated ourselves on the fruits of our misdemeanors.

Waiting for Francie in there ten minutes after stealing the leather jacket, my heart was not pounding. For the first time, I had walked out of the store unafraid of being caught. People always talk about what a rush shoplifting is, but that day, I hadn't been scared and I hadn't been excited. I had just been angry about something that I couldn't name. It wasn't until I was sitting there on the white and gray tile in the wheelchair stall, my back against the partition, that a wave of euphoria rushed over me—a delayed reaction. I had done it. The jacket was mine. I stood up, then sat again, then stood up, then sat. I fiddled with the zipper, trying to find the perfect ratio of leather to cleavage.

When Francie came busting into the stall, I stood one more time.

"My God," she said, out of breath. "You were amazing. Amazing. I couldn't even keep track! I looked away for, like, one second, like, less than a second, and you were gone. The blink of an eye. Amazing!"

I didn't say anything. I stood on my tiptoes and leaned in, and her eyes widened and then closed as I kissed her on the mouth.

Francie's lips were waxy and kiwi-strawberry and I put my hand on hers, my fingertips smooth against her long and shiny nails. Francie, being Francie, made it French. That one time I kissed Francie, fluorescent lights lit us in the bathroom like jellyfish shining miles below everything. And I know what you're thinking, but you're wrong. It wasn't remotely romantic, or even very sexy. But that's not to say it didn't mean anything. Because it did.

It was a pact that bound us. It was a kiss to say, We are deadly. We are sisters. Just to say, Genuine Italian Leather.

Francie with her eyes closed and her tongue cautiously in my mouth. Francie was hot and then she was blinding. Francie was burning and then she was the sun. Francie was the sun and I was—I don't know—something opposite.

Chapter Seven

"Vendela." Ms. Tinker grabbed my arm as I was walking out of class. "I want to talk to you."

"It's Vickie," I corrected her. My name wasn't Vickie, either, but it was what she usually called me, and I had gotten used to it.

"Vendela, Vickie, Velma, Valentina—it's all the same to me," Ms. Tinker said. I think it's possible that she winked when she got to my actual name, but it was hard to be sure, she was such a twitchy person to start with. "I must say that Vendela suits you better than Vickie these days," she went on. "Forgive an old woman for getting mixed up."

Ms. Tinker really wasn't even that old, but she was always acting like she had one foot in the grave. "I'm going to be late to my next class," I told her. I was sick of her bullshit. I zipped my motorcycle jacket all the way to my chin and pulled away. She grabbed me again.

"Hasn't seemed to bother you much lately."

"Can I go?" I asked.

"I'm worried about you," Ms. Tinker said. "Doodles all over your work. Talking back. And you know I don't tolerate tardiness. You used to be one of my best students."

"How could I have been one of your best students? You don't even know my name," I said. I jerked my elbow from her spindly, gnarled hand and pushed out through the door.

At the mall, Francie was making big plans. I sat next to her on the edge of the fountain, half listening as she mused on and on about impossible topics. It was a drone that I liked. The infiniteness of her ambition was reassuring. "We should steal the Holy Grail," she was saying that day, dragging her cupped palm through the water and drawing small whirlpools as she stared into space. "Now that would be a score."

"I doubt they have the Holy Grail at Montgomery Shoppingtowne," I deadpanned. "I definitely haven't spotted it at Wet Seal. Bebe maybe?"

Sarcasm was always lost on Francie. "You never know," she said. "You never know. We haven't even scratched the surface of this place. And if I had the Holy Grail, I'd hide it in an unlikely location. Wouldn't you? I mean, no one's found it yet after, what, two thousand years? It has to be someplace no one's thought to look. What hiding place could be more unlikely than this fake-o palace? Who would ever imagine you could find something real here?"

"There's the Armani store," I said. "That's real Armani."

"Armani Exchange," Francie corrected me. Francie was the type of person who could tell you, in detail, the precise difference between Armani and Armani Exchange, right down to the pattern of the stitching. "A-fucking-X; black ribbed fifty-dollar T-shirt Eurotrash crap. It doesn't count. Face it, Val. There're two and a half real things in this whole entire place. You, me, and the Holy Grail—the Holy Grail only counts half because it's just a suspicion that it's here. And even myself I'm not so sure about all the time, when it comes to realness. Who's to say I'm not a robot, or a hologram? That leaves you."

"Ha!" I said.

"Don't laugh, Val," Francie said. "You are, like, so for real."

If she had told me the same exact thing a few weeks before, I wouldn't have believed her, or even really known what she meant. But sitting there with her, I could feel my blood pumping, pumping against skintight leather. I knew that she was right. "Thanks," I said.

"Well, it's true," she said. "And we're going to find the Holy Grail. I'm not sure why I think it's here, but I do have a feeling." Francie took out her eyeliner and carefully extended her curlicues in a silent show of determination. "My feelings are usually reliable."

"What does the Holy Grail even do, anyway?" I asked. "It has something to do with Indiana Jones, right?"

"Indiana Jones and Jesus," she said. "And it's, like, totally valuable. But the main thing about it is that it lets you live forever. You take a drink from it and *boom*, instant immortality."

"So it's a cup or a mug or something?"

"Well, it's actually technically a *chalice*, I guess, but supposedly it's likely to be enchanted. So maybe it doesn't look like a cup at all. I looked it up on Wikipedia yesterday. There are all kinds of theories. You'd be surprised how much thought people have put into it."

"I bet," I said. I wasn't surprised, though.

"Do you think it's, like, obvious that it's something special?" I asked Francie on a different day. She and I were warming up at Claire's Boutique, digging through wire bins of spray-painted gold junk. "The Holy Grail. Like, could it be disguised as a ball of lint or a piece of toilet paper? That seems like it would be unfair." I palmed a five-dollar package of bangles as I spoke, slipped it in my pocket when I knew no one was looking. It's better to put things in your pocket rather than your bag if you can, because they're less likely to try to search your pockets. Everyone's afraid of lawsuits these days.

"I think whatever it is, it's beautiful," said Francie. "The most beautiful thing. But beautiful in, like, a way that you won't be able to predict. Something you'd think would be nothing, and then you see it and you look carefully, and that's when you're, like, oh my God. I'm pretty sure that's how we'll know."

So we were looking for the Most Beautiful Thing. That was the Holy Grail. The thing you would almost overlook and then, all of a sudden, OMG. I didn't tell Francie why it was so important to me, but I was determined to find it.

Why we thought it was at the mall, I don't know. Francie called it a *suspicion*, but I think it was just the kind of wishful thinking that comes out of shitty circumstance. The J-12 went to Montgomery Shoppingtowne. It didn't go to the Louvre or Vatican City. You believe what you need to believe. So we searched.

And we stole. The two of us, side by side. Me flanking her every move, stealing right while she stole left. We stole Egyptian cotton bedsheets and bottles of perfume and cheap handbags and more costume jewelry than one person could wear in a lifetime. We stole bras and silver-plated pens and Christmas ornaments. With my hair cropped down to messy roots and my motorcycle jacket on, I floated with Francie, for the first time, as an equal.

The Holy Grail turned out to be elusive, though. Every day, after we were finished, we'd make our way to our handicap stall, where we'd take out all our stuff and examine it, just to see if we had found the Grail without realizing it. One time I stole a hundred-dollar pepper grinder that seemed like it had promise. There was something about the way it had called to me in Williams-Sonoma, something about the way it glittered under the soft-focus lighting that made me wonder if it was more than it seemed. But upon examination, in the fluorescence of the bathroom, it was just a regular pepper grinder, and not special at all. It was beyond ordinary— definitely not beautiful.

If you had asked me what the Most Beautiful Thing was, I wouldn't have said it aloud, but secretly I would have known my answer: Francie.

You should understand that she was not exactly a super-model. I mean, she was beautiful, but she wasn't. Yeah, she was tall and blond and booby with amazing legs, but there was something a little funny about her jawline—something square and sharp and almost masculine. Her shoulders were too broad; one eye was just the tiniest bit wonky; her nose had a slight hook; and if you looked closely you could see small blossoms of acne under the crust of her caked-on makeup. It didn't matter. There was just something about her. If you thought too hard about it, she was almost ugly. But then you looked again, and your jaw would drop.

She was a more perfect body pieced together from spares and defectives. From day to day, her appearance was never quite the same. No picture resembled the last. And some-times I wondered if she was replacing her own parts with things she had lifted, one by one. A rhinestone where her left eye should have been. A fist-size crystal paperweight for a heart. It's possible that she was a robot or a hologram. But aren't those things real, too?

I loved Francie. I mean, I was *in* love with Francie. But not in a lesbo way. It wasn't like that. I loved Francie because she had seen something in me that I had never suspected. Because she had unlocked it. She had taught me how to steal. I loved Francie because she was beautiful. Because she was tall. And most of all, because I could not imagine a question that she could not answer. If she didn't know it off the top of her head, she would make something up and be right without even really meaning to be.

Christmas was coming fast. The mall was more jammed every day, and the carols on the sound system got more and more insistent. In the middle of December, it took twenty minutes to make it from Club Libby Lu to Build-a-Bear Workshop; there were just that many people crowding the way. Sitting on the fountain, staring up at the wannabe firmament of tiny white lights strung from skylight to skylight, we imagined ourselves as part of something larger than ourselves.

We were at the Gap ten days before Christmas break, and I had just dropped a lamb's-wool sweater into my bag when I heard my name in a voice I didn't recognize. Shit. I turned around slowly and saw an older, dark-haired girl—in her midtwenties, I figured—standing there, a hand on her hip, kind of smiling at me like we were old friends. I had no idea who she was.

"Val?" she asked. "Is that you?"

"I just want to try it on," I said. "I was just about to go to the dressing room." But the girl gave me a blank look.

"It's me, Liz," she said. "Don't you remember me?"

Then it came to me. It was Liz Jordan, my brother Jesse's old girlfriend from years ago. I couldn't believe that she had recognized me; I'd been just a little kid the last time I'd seen her.

"Hey," I said. I wasn't quite sure how I was supposed to react. "What's up?" I nodded in greeting.

"It *is* you!" she exclaimed. "I can't believe it! Last time I saw you you were, what, ten years old?"

"I guess so," I said. "Or younger?"

Liz squealed and wrapped her arms around me. "It's so awesome to see you! You're all grown-up and everything. You look amazing. Your haircut's awesome!" She pulled away and stood back, regarding me. "I just want to look at you," she said. "Oh my God!" And she ran her fingers across my scalp, mussing what hair I still had.

Francie appeared from wherever she had been. Her earrings were glinting in a way that told me she was saddled down with plenty of loot. She looked from me to Liz and back again. "Hey," she said.

"Francie, this is Liz," I said. "Liz, this is Francie."

Francie looked confused. "Hey," she said. "So, like, how

do you guys know each other? Are you in high school?"

Liz blushed. "I used to date Val's big brother before he turned into a giant homo," Liz informed Francie, who raised an eyebrow. Liz didn't notice, just turned back to me. "Even though, now that I think about it, that was the least of the problem. We're supposedly best friends, but I haven't seen him in, like, at least a year and a half. I mean, we talk on the phone sometimes, but you know how he can be." She cocked her head and put her thumb to her ear, switching into an impersonation of my brother. "'Uh-huh. Yep. Sure. Next week. Yep.'" Liz rolled her eyes. "Like, give me *something*. Just a fucking *word*. It's like he would prefer for no one to care about him. Well, sorry, but I'm your fucking best friend, Jesse."

"You sound like my mom," I said. "Except that my mom doesn't actually say any of that."

"Ha. Well, maybe that's why he doesn't like talking to me. Whatever. He's doing better these days, right?"

"It's not like I would know. Last I heard, he was living in Harlem with some sixty-year-old dude."

"Oh, that was ages ago, thank God," Liz said. "Ambrose. That guy was a real creep. Anyway, I do think he's doing better. Him coming home is, like, a good sign, I'm pretty sure. But really, you can't try to speculate; you'll be wrong every time. We won't know for sure until he's back for Christmas, I guess."

I did a double take. "He's coming home for Christmas?"

"Uh, duh!" Liz said. "Where have you been?" Then she jerked her head and looked around the overrun store, distracted. Clothes were strewn on the floor and jumbled in huge messy piles on top of the tables. There didn't seem to be a single folded garment in the entire place. "God, this place is a dump," she said. "Back to work, I guess."

"You work here?" Francie asked.

Liz rolled her eyes. "I'm the assistant manager. Maybe you should just kill me now." Then she walked off to fold some clothes and called over her shoulder to me. "I'm sure I'll see you when he's back in town. I missed you!"

"We need to get out of here, like, *now*," Francie muttered. She shot a suspicious look at Liz Jordan's back and took my hand, marching me out of the store, back into the mall, where we were swallowed up by the crowd. We stood alone in the center of the atrium while people streamed around us.

"What the fuck!" Francie said. "You didn't tell me you have a brother! Do you seriously have a brother?"

"He's not like a regular brother," I said.

"Clearly." Francie snorted. "I mean, really, for fuck's sake! How do you have a brother and not even mention it? Anything else you're not telling me?"

"He's dying," I said. "Like, any day now."

Francie stared at me. "Seriously?"

I nodded.

"That's so shitty," she said.

"Yeah," I said. "It's really shitty."

"Well," Francie decided, "if he's coming home for Christmas, we need to get him presents." Francie was always so practical like that.

My older brother was dying. No one had ever told me that he was dying; I'd been forced to figure it out on my own. I didn't know exactly what his problem was except that it didn't seem like a normal disease or anything like that. It seemed like something almost mystical. A problem that only the Holy Grail might be able to solve. Not that I believed in things like that.

I mean, I only believed in them a little. I wasn't sure exactly what I believed in anymore. But I believed in Francie. I believed in my motorcycle jacket. And I believed that when it comes to things like the Holy Grail, people are usually willing to bend their beliefs.

"What would he want?" Francie wondered aloud. She worried the middle of her forehead with an index finger. "Is he into video games?" she asked hopefully.

"Not that I know of," I said.

"Hmm," Francie said. She knitted her brows together, just slightly disgruntled. "I thought that video games were what brothers liked. Well, we'll think of something."

Francie would think of something. Francie always had the answers. I had questions. The question I wanted to ask but didn't was this one: How do you rebuild a boy? I figured that if anyone could tell me, it was Francie.

We went to J.Crew and stole Jesse a pair of plaid footy pajamas—"So cute," according to Francie—and then moved on to Hollister, for a long-sleeve T that said *HOLLISTER* on it, and finally back to Crate & Barrel, where I took a Marimekko platter with a kind of paisley print, still for him.

Francie approved. "Everyone loves platters," she pronounced. "They always come in handy. You have to let me sign the card."

"Sure," I said.

"A present that is stolen means more. It shows you're really willing to take a risk for someone else."

"I thought people liked it when you spent money on them," I said.

"Yeah, but that's different. When you steal something for someone, you put yourself on the line. And it's like, by risking your own safety, you're tapping into this, like, infinite life force of the universe, taking just a little piece and giving it to someone else."

"That makes no sense at all," I said.

"It's just what I believe," Francie told me.

At the dinner table that night, my mom sat to my left and my asshole stepfather, Jack, to my right, all of us crunching away at our salads and not saying anything. We never had a lot to say. It wasn't that my mom and I didn't like each other. It was just that she had other things on her mind. She was distracted by something, and had been for several years. But she was also really into totally pointless things like Family Dinner, no matter how excruciating it was for everyone.

"You didn't tell me Jesse was coming home for Christmas," I said after a while.

My mom looked up. "What are you talking about?" she asked.

"Jesse. Christmas," I said. "How come you didn't tell me?"

"Who said your brother's coming home for Christmas?" she asked. Jack said nothing, but I registered a look of disturbance on his face. He had a piece of half-chewed lettuce dangling from the corner of his mouth. Gross.

"I saw that girl Liz at the mall. She told me. Does anyone know anything around here?" I snapped my fingers around my face, like, *Hellooo*.

"Don't talk to your mother like that," Jack said. I gave him the smarmiest smile I could muster.

"Well, it's all news to me," my mom said. She seemed hesitant to take me seriously.

I stood up and left the table without saying anything, and went outside to the front yard where I sat on the curb, even though it was December and getting really cold. I folded my knees to my chest and wrapped my arms around my legs. I wanted a cigarette, but I didn't have any. Instead, I puffed my chest and blew, and watched my breath expel in round puffs of steam. It was almost like smoking if you didn't think too hard about it.

My family was so fucked up. When Jesse had been around it was always some imagined disaster or another, but now it was just this overwhelming, impenetrable *nothing*. Sometimes it seemed like you could go days in my house without hearing any noise except the buzz of the television from the den and, once in a while, a door easing shut.

I don't remember my real dad. He left when I was really little and I guess it was just as well, anyway, because from what I've gathered he was a total asshole. My mom married Jack next, and he was a disaster, too. He's, like, the king of all dicks, but I guess I just learned to ignore it and go about my business. My brother had never picked up on that skill. He had hated Jack with a passion from the moment he'd laid eyes on him and had never let up. I guess it will mess a nine-year-old boy up when his real dad drops off the face of the planet, and then mess him up even more when that sucky dad is replaced by an even more sucky one. I guess it's just, like, What is the point of any of this? Eventually Jesse decided, like my father, that there wasn't a point at all, and left. First home, then town.

Mom hadn't been the same since he'd gone. She had just given up, I think. I couldn't remember the last time she had raised her voice about anything. I couldn't remember the last time she had been interested in anything anyone had to say. She could see that everything was totally fucked, but she couldn't summon the strength it took to change it.

I hated her, I realized. I hated her.

I listened to the buzz of a flickering streetlight directly above my head and felt a recklessness of ambition tingling in my gut. I wanted, more than anything, to be different from my mother, who was the kind of person who saw that there was a thunderstorm and went out without an umbrella anyway, because it seemed futile trying to stay dry so why bother.

I wanted something different for myself. Suddenly I could see possibility everywhere, and I knew that to ignore it was the height of spinelessness. Francie had taught me that.

Just earlier that day, I'd thought I wanted to be like Francie, but that wasn't it. Well, it was and it wasn't. I did want to be like Francie, but sitting there on the curb outside my house, I knew that it went further than that. I wanted more. There was so much more to want. I wanted everything.

Chapter Eight

Francie disappeared without explanation the day before winter break. She wasn't in school, and her cell phone went straight to voice mail when I tried to call her. When I hadn't heard from her three days later, right before Christmas Eve, I thought about going by the house on Maple to see if there was anyone there, and then decided against it. I didn't want to be a stalker. With nothing to do, I occupied myself by lying on my bed and listening to music on my headphones, staring at the ceiling and thinking, wondering what I might have done to piss her off. I worried that I hadn't done anything, and that was the worst possibility of all. What if she had come to her senses, had just suddenly realized what I had suspected since the beginning: that I was not at all what she had expected me to be.

Wasn't I, though? I wasn't who I had been. That much I knew for sure. The girl in the back of the classroom was gone forever—I remembered her like a cousin I'd known as a little kid and had fallen away from as we'd gotten older. But with that girl gone for good, I was uncertain who had replaced her. Because lying there on my bed, with my headphones on, Francie who knew where, I could feel myself scattering, the edges of myself blurring into limitless dark. I could feel myself grasping for my own name. Vendela? Vickie? Valerie?

I thought I had changed. I had cut my hair, learned to steal, changed everything about myself. Now, with Francie gone, I had to wonder if I'd just been imagining things. Was I just a question mark without her?

If she had been there with me, she would have taken me by the wrists and shaken me, laughing. Would have told me to stop feeling sorry for myself. Or said, "Please, Val, don't you think you're overthinking things?" Or maybe she wouldn't have needed to say anything.

Because sometimes, after trips to the mall, Francie and I would go back to her house and not even talk. She'd turn on Prince or Joy Division or the Aztec Camera or whatever band she was obsessed with at the moment, and we'd just lie on her bed. Her chain-smoking with her laptop balanced on her thighs, sending prank messages to strangers on MySpace and laughing to herself, and me looking through *Vanity Fair* or whatever, maybe reading the horoscopes out loud but otherwise quiet. Stealing a drag off her cigarette from time to time. We didn't need to say anything. We had a kingdom, even if it was just the two of us, and in the throne room of Francie's bedroom, we'd been untouchable and ultimate.

The point wasn't the talking, and it wasn't quite the smoking, either, because I wasn't actually into the smoking part of smoking. I thought it tasted gross, plus it made me lightheaded. Despite what my health teacher insisted, I wasn't doing it to be cool. I just liked the feeling of being with Francie, sharing something intimate and quiet. Smoking with Francie, me on her swivel chair and her on top of her duvet in nothing but fancy lace underwear and green rubber Wellingtons—which she liked to wear for no reason when the mood struck her—I sometimes stared at the smoke drifting, the light catching it in its intricate, ghostly spiral, and felt bodiless, like maybe we had stepped outside of the normal flow of everything. Like, as long as the cigarette was burning the Earth might continue to rotate while Francie and I stayed casually fixed in one universal location.

With Francie, in her room, I knew who I was. I knew what I was supposed to be. In Francie's room I could see my world set out in front of me as a simple, perfect scheme.

Now she was gone, and I felt myself going.

But a funny thing happened. At almost the exact moment that Francie vanished, my brother rematerialized—showed up on Christmas Eve, just like Liz said he would. A click at the door, and then he was stepping inside, like no time had passed. Like it was nothing at all. That was just Jesse.

On Christmas Eve, when Jesse walked through the door, he didn't have to say a word. He dropped his old keys on the front table, and then my mom was running from the kitchen like a cat who's heard the crunch of a can opener. Jesse just stood there, with that old *who me?* look on his face, the furrow of mock apology he'd perfected as a teenager, and my mom threw her arms around him, sniffling, and he looked over and winked at me as if to tell me I was the only person in the world who was in on his conspiracy. Everything felt pretty normal for a second. We hadn't seen him for close to two years.

Jesse was handsome. He had always been handsome, and he would always be handsome. Even when he was at his sickest, it had manifested itself—in terms of his appearance—as a fashionable wasting. Cheekbones, cheekbones, cheekbones. Now, in a ratty, pilled cashmere sweater and a pair of tattered jeans, he looked like a teen idol who had hit hard times. It was an improvement over the last time I'd seen him, but still. His face was drawn, his hair was patchy, and his eyes had sunk deep into his face. His beard was scraggly and uneven.

It was always hard to tell how serious things really were with him. He had been sick for four years, but I sometimes wondered if it had been longer than that. If he had been sick for forever. There was something that was so mysterious about the whole thing—it was more like a curse than an illness. Like he'd been born under a dark and reckless star.

When my mom finally let him go, Jesse turned to me and gave me an awkward kiss with icy lips. He had to really hunch to reach my cheek, and his bag swung around and hit me in the side.

"Hey," I said.

"Is this my same little sister?" he asked. I shrugged like I didn't know what he was talking about, but I was happy that he had noticed the change.

I didn't talk to Jesse much that day. My mom wouldn't let him out of her sight, and I couldn't deal with listening to her grill him for information that we all knew he'd never give up. Jack knew that he wasn't really welcome where Jesse was concerned, so he was keeping to himself, too, holed up in the basement in front of the television.

I spent hours wrapping and rewrapping my Christmas presents, making sure the creases in the paper were all scored perfectly, that all patterns matched up exactly where the ends met. Everything tight and straight and absolutely flawless. Beautiful.

When I was finally finished, I walked to 7-Eleven and bought a pack of Marlboro Lights, then headed down to the creek by myself, where I sat shivering and smoking until it was almost dark. I wondered where Francie was. I wondered where my brother had been for the last couple of years. New York, okay, but beyond that he had never really bothered to tell. It was no surprise. That's how he had always been.

Jesse had always been so much older than me. He was nine years old when I was born. I knew him first as a teenager, when he had seemed constantly engaged in some larger battle that I couldn't know. He was always ready to attack: ears pricked, ropy muscles coiled and twitching.

Practically the only thing I remembered about my brother living at home were his fights with my stepfather, over who-knows-what and probably nothing, both of them screaming and throwing things across the room at each other, my mother sitting on the kitchen floor looking hopeless, running her fingers anxiously through her hair, and then Jesse just walking out the door. He always showed back up on the threshold a few days later looking sheepish and none the worse for wear, backpack drooping from his shoulder and chin cocked at a dopey angle that suggested contrition. But he never actually said he was sorry, and he never told anyone where it was he had been. Probably he wasn't sorry, and maybe there's part of the story that no one told me. I was really just a kid back then.

He'd been mean. He'd gone years barely acknowledging me at all, except to grab the remote control while I was trying to watch television. One time, when I was six or seven years old, he threw that same remote at my head and missed, grazing my scalp and shattering a window. He was a dick. His nickname for me was the Little Shit.

But then sometimes, at the beach on rare family vacations, he would carry me on his back into the ocean, out past where I could stand, and I'd float while he shaped my hair into saltwater sculptures, singing under his breath, "Yellow is the color of my true love's hair . . ." even though my hair wasn't yellow. That was why I loved him.

This is nothing new, I know. This is an older brother.

On Christmas morning, Jesse cut his eyes in my direction when my mom opened the Swarovski unicorn figurine I'd gotten for her, and then again and with a raised eyebrow when Jack opened that stupid pepper grinder from Williams-Sonoma. Mom and Jack seemed to appreciate the gifts but didn't have a lot to say about them. When we got to the stuff that Francie and I had gotten for my brother, Jesse just tore into them, tossing crumpled paper at his feet. His face was mottled with the glow of the tiny white lights on the tree, and as he examined each present, I could see something returning to him, his cheeks reddening, shoulders perking up. The Christmas lights dimmed, just barely, as his eyes widened and twinkled.

"Footy pajamas!" Jesse said, truly happy. He smiled up at me, and for the first time in as long as I could possibly remember, he looked healthy. "You're the best," he said, kissing me. His lips felt warm on my cheek. And I thought about what Francie had said when we'd left the mall with his gifts in hand. *A gift that is stolen means more*. It had seemed like just another one of her silly, overdramatic pronouncements. But the fact is that when Jesse had kissed me two days ago, I'd questioned whether he had a pulse left at all. Now I could feel his blood pumping.

Jesse's gift for me was a small leather notebook. Apparently his friend in New York made them and sold them on consignment in fancy little shops. It was nice, even though I couldn't think what I'd write in it.

But then, after breakfast and back in my room, I took the notebook out, ran my fingers over the blank pulpy pages, and finally took out a pink jelly-roll pen and wrote, in perfectly neat and tiny handwriting:

1) Leather motorcycle jacket
2) Dior eyeliner, liquid
3) Swarovski unicorn sculpture

I kept going, listing the things I had stolen one by one. It wasn't everything—I was sure I was forgetting stuff here and there—but it was a start. I decided that from then on I would catalog everything I shoplifted in the little leather notebook. A record is important for various reasons. Even when it comes to crime.

When I was done, I looked down and back over what I had written. And with the beginning right there on paper, I had a funny thought: Where is the end? As a rational person you know that every road leads eventually to some depressing, tacky cul-de-sac. But at that point I could not imagine that I would ever stop stealing. I could not imagine that my brother would die. Even with all evidence to the contrary, with Francie so far out of pocket, I could not imagine that she and I would ever not be friends.

The next day, Jesse and I finally had a chance to talk. He grabbed me by the elbow when I was standing in front of the open refrigerator and dragged me out to Mom's old Ford Taurus. "Quick, before she notices I'm gone," he said.

It was cold out but not too cold. Inside the car, Jesse blasted the heat and rolled the windows down, turned the radio up. We took the parkway along the creek, heading nowhere specific as far as I could tell.

"So you've taken up shoplifting," Jesse said. He had one hand on the wheel and another dangling out the window with a cigarette. He kept both eyes on the road. "Either that or dealing drugs. But let's face it, you're not the drug dealer type. That statue thing you got Mom must have cost at least a couple hundred dollars."

"Three," I said. I was too surprised to play dumb. "So? It's not like she even noticed."

"Then you admit it," he said.

"What, like you're a cop now?"

"I'm not going to tell on you. I'm just curious. Liz and I used to be pretty amazing shoplifters, you know."

"You're forgetting that I don't know the first thing about you, really," I said. He looked at me like I had honestly wounded him, and I felt kind of bad. It was true, though.

The details of my brother's life had always been entirely mysterious. "So you used to steal?" I asked.

"Yeah," he said. "Liz got me into it, but in the end I was even better than she was."

"It must run in the family."

"I guess so. And wanna hear something weird? I used to imagine I was a girl when I did it. For some reason that made it easier—if that's not totally the queerest thing ever."

I snorted like it was without a doubt the queerest thing I'd ever heard in my life, but the truth was that it made total and perfect sense. "Well, girls are better thieves," I said. "Everyone knows that. Anyway, I seriously doubt you could have been as good as me and Francie," I told him. "We can steal anything."

"Just don't get caught," Jesse said. "Over five hundred dollars is a felony. As in you go to jail. Or at least court. Also not fun. Who's Francie?"

"She's this girl," I said. "I mean, she's my friend, I think. Long story, basically."

"Tell," Jesse said. And I told him the whole story—how I had met Francie, how she had taught me how to shoplift, how she'd changed my life, and how she'd disappeared.

It had started to flurry, and with no place to go we were now driving in circles, back and forth, up and down the parkway. No one else was on the road. "Sometimes people have shit to take care of," Jesse said.

"You would know about that."

"Ouch!" Jesse said.

"Well, it's true," I said. This time I didn't really care if I hurt his feelings.

"I'll explain someday," he told me.

When we got home, we poured ourselves bowls of cereal, went down to the basement, and kicked Jack off the television. There was a *Designing Women* marathon on Lifetime, and we basically didn't get up off the couch for the next couple of days. It made me nearly forget that Francie was gone. But not quite.

Chapter Nine

rancie came back. You knew she would.

She returned on the last day of winter break, appeared there on the doorstep, just like Jesse. Francie was shivering cold, a pink cashmere scarf thrown around her neck but otherwise dressed completely inappropriately for the weather—really, for almost any occasion—in a black sequined off-the-shoulder dress with a chiffon bubble skirt. Bare arms and no jacket in thirty-degree weather. At least she was wearing tights.

Francie had never been to my house before, and I'm not exactly sure how she even knew where it was. I guess it wasn't too hard to figure out. Jesse beat me to the door to let her in. He had been expecting Liz all morning, and he'd been waiting on the couch in the living room next to the front door, pretending to read *The New York Times Magazine* but definitely anxious, fidgeting and adjusting and flipping back and forth between the same two pages for at least an hour. He'd cleaned himself up for her, which was weird to me, because he was the one who had dumped her, years ago, to become a fag. So why should he care whether he looked good or not? But he did.

I watched him meet Francie from the landing on the stairs, and it was easy to see from the way her face changed that she fell in love with him the moment she laid eyes on him. Even though I couldn't see Jesse's expression, I had a feeling that he fell for her, too. I didn't really know Jesse that well, but he was still my brother, and I knew him enough to understand that the flagrant, almost ceremonial gesture of Francie's insane outfit would appeal to him.

Francie liked him, obviously, because he was cute.

"I'm a friend of Val's," she said. She kissed Jesse on the cheek and stepped inside without being invited. He stood there with his hand still on the doorknob and waited a pointed beat before turning to me, still on the landing, meeting my eyes with an expression like *You've got to be kidding* but at the same time totally charmed and *I love her already*.

Francie hadn't spotted me yet. She was standing in the foyer fidgeting with my mom's tchotchkes on the front table, not quite sure of the etiquette of what to do next. Jesse just looked at her with good-natured bemusement.

Francie seemed, uncharacteristically, to be avoiding eye contact with him.

"Hey, bitch," I said after a while.

Francie looked up with starry, charmed openness, shrugged happily, and made a kissy-face. "Hey, bitch," she said.

I wanted to be pissed at her. Because where had she been and why hadn't she called me? But with the feeling of relief I had, watching her standing there in my house for the first time, out of her element like I'd never seen her before, I just had to laugh and bound down the stairs and throw my arms around her.

"Where have you been?" I asked, kissing her on the cheek.

"You know Sandy. The day before Christmas, she just, like, decides we're going to the Bahamas, like *right now*. We didn't even have tickets when we got to the airport—we bought them at the counter. That woman is crazy. It's a good thing she's rich, because I don't know how we'd survive otherwise. She'd probably be sponging off of me instead of off her parents. I'd be working in a cannery or a paper mill or something. Imagine what it would do to my complexion!"

Jesse laughed in that stuttery way that was kind of a hiccup, like it had caught him by surprise, a completely reflexive response. "Not your complexion!" he said, clasping his chest. Francie looked like she couldn't decide whether to be embarrassed or pleased by his reaction. She tossed her hair and batted her eyelashes. We headed down to the basement, and Jesse followed, unable to resist Francie's lure.

"Val never talks about you," Francie babbled. "It's, like, this whole mystery or something. Man, it is freezing out there. So what's your deal, anyway?"

"My deal?" asked Jesse.

"I'm not trying to be rude or anything; I'm just curious," Francie said.

"It's kind of a long story," Jesse said, and changed the subject. "So I hear you've introduced my sister into a life of crime."

Francie blushed and giggled. "Uh, I don't know what you're talking about. Do you guys have the Game of Life? I love that one. I love how you get to have those funny babies in the back of the car."

I pulled the Game of Life down from the top shelf of the basement closet and spread out the pieces on the gray-blue wall-to-wall carpeting.

Liz showed up a half hour later. We were still sitting on the floor in the basement playing the game when she arrived; she just walked in and came straight downstairs without knocking. I guess that even after all these years she knew our family well enough to know that any form of politesse would be completely wasted on us.

"I'm pink," Liz said, before even saying hello. Jesse just started laughing, and she slid in next to him on the floor and mussed his hair and kissed him on the forehead. He really did look happy.

"You look great," Liz said. "I mean, you look like a new man."

"I'm feeling a lot better these days," Jesse said. "I mean, these days as in the past couple of days. I had to leave New York. Being back here—it's like overnight everything's so much better. Ever since Christmas."

Francie gave me a curious look.

"New York will fuck you up," Liz said.

"Wait, so you're staying?" I asked.

"I moved back into my old place," he said. "The girl who was subletting got knocked up and moved in with her boyfriend. It's gonna be just like old times."

"Great," Liz said uncertainly. She was counting her cash, and I watched her. I remembered her from the old days in only the vaguest terms: as an intimidating presence that seemed to hold keys to vaults of uncharted knowledge. But now, watching her shuffle those pastel bills in her hand, then reshuffle them, then count them off one more time, I saw something in her tentativeness that indicated she was really just as lost as anyone else.

"So I hear you got a job at the Gap," Jesse said.

"Ugh," Liz said. "Don't remind me—assistant manager. So insanely boring, but a job's a job. And the whole famous actress thing really wasn't working out in LA."

"Montgomery Shoppingtowne," Jesse said. "Better watch

out for thieves. I hear they have a problem with thievery at Montgomery Shoppingtowne." He smirked to himself, and Francie shot me a look.

Liz just rolled her eyes. "Yeah. How's that sweater, anyway, Val?"

I laughed nervously.

"Listen, if someone actually wants that crap they can help themselves. I could give you some pointers, though." She looked over at Francie. "Jesse and I used to be the best shoplifters around. I was, like, the queen of all shoplifters."

Francie made the Sign, but Liz just looked at her like she was insane. Francie shrugged at me like, *Well, I tried.* And Liz spun the wheel, moved her car across the board, and drew a card. "Yay, I won the Nobel Prize!" she said, helping herself to a pile of cash from the bank. "I always knew I was destined for something bigger."

When we were bored with the Game of Life, Jesse went upstairs and snuck a couple bottles of chardonnay and brought them back down for the four of us to pass around among ourselves. Francie and I lay toe-to-toe together, perpendicular on the sectional sofa, mostly listening to Liz and Jesse and only chiming in occasionally. For the first time in ages, maybe ever, I felt like I had a real family. Looking at them—the way they looked at each other, the casual way Jesse's big toe rubbed Liz's ankle, the two of them sprawled on the carpet—I wished Jesse and Liz were my parents. I wondered what would have happened if things weren't the way they were. If maybe she could have averted his various disasters.

When it had been dark for several hours, Francie stood. You could see she was a little drunk, but just a little. "I should go," she said. "My mom hates being home alone, especially at night. It makes her go kind of insane."

"So what did you think of Francie?" I asked Jesse after she left.

"She didn't get much of a tan in the Bahamas," he said.

Chapter Ten

There was always something different about the mall. As well as you thought you knew it, it was never what you remembered. At the mall, you'd put one foot in front of the other only to look over your shoulder and realize that the path you had been following had rearranged itself behind your back.

Stores that were there one minute would be gone the next, replaced by something new and even less practical. In the blink of an eye, Everything Buckets became Eyelash Bar. Francie and I liked Eyelash Bar for a lot of reasons, not the least or most of which was the stupid name. Anyway, who doesn't sometimes need fake eyelashes?

The mall had a way of giving you what you wanted. It

had a way of reflecting back what you gave it. But you had to know how to read the signs.

Sometimes I dreamed about the mall. In the dream, which was the same every time, I stepped alone from the glass elevator onto a fourth level that didn't exist, to find a new storefront that I'd seen before in other dreams, but which surprised me every time anyway. The store was called the Thieves' Guild. It sold things like lockpicks and walkie talkies and professional-grade booster bags and those little stethoscopes that you use to listen for the clicks on combination locks. Other than the unusual selection of merchandise, the Thieves' Guild looked about the same as any other third-rate mall store. Not quite as nice as Spencer Gifts and not quite as crappy as Dollar Bin, the Thieves' Guild had tightly packed shelves and wall-to-wall carpeting and cameras pointed haphazardly in every direction, probably recording nothing. Francie was the manager of the store, and even dream-Francie couldn't be bothered, I'm sure, to do something so pointless as change tapes in surveillance cameras. Instead, she sat behind the counter, painstakingly working on her makeup without the aid of a mirror, making such tiny strokes with her eyebrow pencil that you could barely tell her fingers were moving. Dream-Francie wore a white catsuit and a gold chain necklace with a giant diamond pendant that dangled suggestively between her breasts. Her hair was even longer and crazier than usual—it hung almost to her ankles and was sort of alive, twisting and hissing like a nest of snakes. Sometimes she was disguised as Ursula Andress, depending on which angle you caught her from, but even with her in disguise, there could be no confusion about the fact that it was Francie.

Francie in the dream didn't remember me, but she liked me anyway—I could tell from the way her diamond sparkled. Dream-Francie didn't speak.

In the dream, every time, I approached Francie at the cash register, and she tugged at her earlobes and wiggled her nose. When I made the Sign back to her, she beckoned to me wordlessly from behind the counter and gestured to a small trapdoor under her feet. She stepped aside, daring me, and I crawled onto the floor and opened the door, and jumped into an unknown—only to find myself standing on a stuttering escalator in another mall. A cleaner, brighter mall where everything was new and everyone looked happy. At the other mall, they sold the one thing that I needed. And I didn't even have to steal it, because it was on clearance for the low price of Free. When the alarm clock rang, I could never remember what that one thing was.

In my dreams, in real life, the mall was always trying to tell me something. It was hard to say exactly what, but one thing was for sure: the mall was more than it appeared. No matter how run-down and depressing it sometimes was, with empty storefronts always popping up to be converted into gloomy "hospitality lounges" with a couple of raggedy office chairs and a fake tree, the mall would always absorb the loss and come back with something else worth stealing. Something you had to have. The Most Beautiful Thing.

Because the mall wanted to live. The mall would live. And the mall had intentions of its own. You had to wonder if it was setting up dominoes when it delivered Max to us.

Francie and I were smoking in a corner by our emergency exit, the empty part of the parking garage, when he first appeared. It was unseasonably warm for January, and we'd had a big day. Francie had scored herself an iPod from JCPenney by hiding it in a cheap nylon duffel bag and then buying the duffel bag. She'd hidden it on a Monday and come back to complete the scheme on a Friday, a technique she'd read about on the internet. It wasn't the same as stealing it outright, because she was actually spending money, but it was still a net profit of almost three hundred dollars, if you wanted to look at it that way. And even if you didn't look at it that way, it was still worth it.

Francie had just unfolded the instructions for the iPod when there was a clackety-clack in the distance. We both looked up, startled. There was never, ever anyone else in the Q section of the parking lot. But that day, suddenly, there was a blur flying around the corner, and a crash, and then, truly out of nowhere, this guy was lying on the ground fifteen yards away in a tangled heap. His skateboard kept rolling without him and settled curiously at my feet like a puppy.

"Things are always getting more interesting," Francie said.

The boy was lying there, eyes clenched, muscles cramped up in pain.

I looked at Francie. She raised her eyebrows. I reached down to pick up the skateboard, but it was too late. Francie had already tucked it under her arm and was standing up.

"Shall we check it out?" she asked. It was rhetorical; here was a boy, all wounded and sexy and everything, lying on the ground and waiting for us to come along and nurse him back to health. Obviously the answer was yes. And then she was marching over to him.

I half didn't want to follow her. The skateboard had landed at my feet, not hers. She should have been the one following me. But everything was always meant for Francie; I knew that, too. The idea that something could have been mine by rights would never have occurred to her.

So I followed her anyway.

We stood over the guy and looked at him curiously. He was our age, probably, and kinda hot, I think. I mean, it looked like he was maybe hot. It was actually hard to tell because his face was all screwed up in pain. He was hugging his knee to his chest and writhing.

"Are you okay?" asked Francie. "I brought your skateboard." She dropped it at his side, and it hung there, tentative. Without meaning to, I rolled my eyes.

"Thanks," he said. "Give me a second. Ouch." It looked like maybe he was crying, or about to start.

It occurred to me that we should leave and come back—

give him some privacy—but Francie waited, patient and expectant, while he wheezed, and I stood with her, feeling dumb. Finally he sat up and propped himself on his hands. "Hey," he said. "Sorry. I thought my leg was broken for a second there. But I'm fine."

"Hey," I said.

"I'm Francie. This is Valentina," Francie said. Sometimes she really had no sense of shame.

"I'm Max," Max said. He stood up, and I realized that I had been right: he was totally hot, with scruffy sandy hair and blue eyes, his tight, vintagey T-shirt straining at his biceps. It was unseasonably warm out, but not really warm enough for a T-shirt, and I noticed the blond hairs on the backs of his arms standing on end.

"Nice moves you got there," Francie said. Max looked her up and down, took in the whole picture. Francie had her hair piled into an enormous, teased beehive that day, and the effect was quite something.

"Uh," Max said, "nice to meet you." Then he picked up his board and skated the hell out of there before Francie could open her mouth again.

"That was a success," I said. I could still hear the rattling of Max's skateboard in the distance, getting fainter.

"Just wait," Francie said. "If you love something, set it free. He'll be back."

We went to visit Liz at the Gap. "Welcome to the Gap," Liz said when we walked in. "My name's Liz. What can I help you find today?" She smiled with exaggerated conde-scension. Without taking her eyes off of us, she knocked a pile of sweaters onto the floor and walked away.

"She'll be getting that promotion to general manager any day now," Francie muttered. She pulled a tube of lip gloss out of her bag and glopped an oily blob onto her mouth.

It was pretty obvious that Liz was bored out of her mind. She was perched on a stepladder now, fiddling with her two-way headset. "Breaker, breaker to Dixie Cup!" she was saying. "Dixie Cup, you got a smokey in a brown wrap-per knocking at your back door, you copy?"

You could see the clerks rolling their eyes at one another from opposite ends of the store.

"You're going to get fired if you don't shape up," Francie informed her. "I mean, this isn't exactly profes-sional behavior."

"These clowns get what they pay for," Liz said. "I barely make more than an associate!"

"Don't they get mad at you, though?" I asked.

"I'm a totally different person when the general man-ager's around," she said. "So professional. How's your brother?"

"I don't know. Good, I guess," I told her. "I haven't seen too much of him since Christmas. He, like, disappeared again. I'm glad he's better, though."

"Are you sure he's better?"

"What's even *wrong* with him?" Francie demanded.

"People keep talking about how sick he is, but he seemed fine to me! Will someone please fill me in?"

"He's dying," I said. "Things were bad, but now I guess he's better."

"He's not better," said Liz. "I mean, I've been burned by thinking that way in the past. You think he's all fine again and then *wham*. I keep calling him, but does he call me back?"

Liz left the answer unsaid, but Francie's mind was elsewhere anyway. "Have you ever seen him naked?" she asked me.

"Ugh!" I gagged.

"What?" Francie said. "He's hot as hell! What's so wrong about that?"

"He's my brother!" I said.

"Exactly," said Francie. "So you must have seen him coming out of the shower. Or something. Right?"

"Wrong!" Francie could be truly disgusting sometimes.

"Well, I've seen him naked," Liz said. "Even if it was a long time ago. And he *is* hot."

"Ugh!" I said. "Please!"

"Here," Liz said. She took a pair of dark, stiff jeans off the denim wall, and without even bothering to check if anyone was looking, opened my bag to drop them in. "Those will fit him," she said. "Use them as an excuse to visit him, and tell him I say hi."

"Thanks," I said.

We left the store, and the mall whirled around us—like it

was thinking hard, considering all possible outcomes. The Gap became Waldenbooks became Pottery Barn became Candy Express became Tuesday Morning. I snapped the rubber bands around my wrist to keep from getting disoriented.

"See?" Francie said. "Liz knows it, too. She doesn't know about the Sign, but even she knows that a stolen gift is something special."

"Do you think we'll ever see him again?" I asked Francie.

"Of course. It's not like he's in Timbuktu. I mean, it's not like he's even in New York! He's a couple of stops away on the subway. You guys are so weird about him. Come on—you could go there right now, if that was what you wanted."

"I wasn't talking about my brother," I said. For less than a split second, I had the impression that Francie and I were standing in a ruin: that the mall had crumbled around us, and it was just Francie and me with dirt and ancient, weathered marble tiles under our spike heels. A brittle potted palm stood alone a few feet off, pathetic and withered and yellowed by time. I caught my breath and the mall sprung up again, reconstructed itself in the blink of an eye, brick by brick, into a bright and glittering temple that was even better than it had been to start with.

"Oh," Francie said. "I should have known. You were talking about *him*."

"Yeah," I said.

"I wouldn't worry about it," Francie said. "I told you, he'll be back."

Her dangly silver fishtail earrings were throwing flash everywhere, and it was obvious what she was thinking. She was thinking she could have anything she wanted. All she had to do was want it and it was hers.

Before heading home, Francie and I stepped onto the elevator together—the same elevator that was in my dream. In the glass chamber, our reflections were gilded in gold, and they stared back at us, transfixed, as the food court receded and the uppermost tier of the mall approached. That day, instead of turning to me, Francie spoke to my reflection, and said, "You're my best friend. You know that, right?"

"Of course," my reflection said.

"I have your back," she said. "Do you have mine?"

"I will always have your back," I told Francie. And I meant it. Of course I meant it.

Francie could do this. She could be bossy, selfish, thoughtless, bug the crap out of me. And then, just like that, she would remind me of not just everything that she had given me, but everything she would always give. Her irrational, unquenchable generosity. A lock of hair had worked its way out of her beehive and was curling around her jaw.

Francie grabbed my hand. It was the real Francie now, no reflection, and my real actual hand. She squeezed it, hard. It was then, feeling her inch-long, foil-plated nails digging into my knuckles, that I knew that Francie was not exaggerating at all. Maybe Francie never exaggerated. She did have my back. She would not let anything hurt me. She had said it over and over again; it was important to her in a way that I could never totally understand. The way it meant something to her, I knew I could never, ever match.

Chapter Eleven

The fountain was holding the whole thing together. From a perch on the edge of it, in the middle of the mall's central hub, you could skim your fingers along the surface of the water and look around and see every aspect. The vantage allowed for an unsettling feeling of omniscience, the way a simple swivel in any direction presented another tableau. The Trench Coat Mafia loitering outside Hot Topic, pretending to be dangerous; the Caribbean nannies wandering out of the Gap and yapping at each other over giant strollers. From the fountain, you could just shift your gaze to another cluster and understand not only who they were but know instinctively exactly what they were saying to each other.

Even the few parts of Montgomery Shoppingtowne that

you couldn't actually see: sitting at the fountain, it was like you had this awareness. Like you were somehow plugged into the nervous system. The water bubbling, the lights shining up from the bottom. Country club blue. Scrape the tiles with your fingers, sift through pennies. Francie and I could both feel Max heading toward us, I think. We looked at each other. Francie smiled an *I told you so* and quickly wiped a small trace of Cinnabon icing from the corner of her mouth. She patted down her hair.

And then he was sitting next to us. Just slid right in, all cool like that. "Hey, ladies," he said.

"Hey," I said. He was looking at Francie.

"Max!" she said. As if she was surprised. She ran a finger around the edge of her ear, along her cheekbone to her jaw, and then, tilting her chin, down her long neck and across her bare collarbone.

"You remembered my name," Max said.

"Duh," Francie said. "How could we forget?"

Max had a nose you could write a poem about. I would write a poem about it myself if I was the kind of person who knew how to do things like write poems. Well, it was a nose like a cat's. Broad and flat but strong, too; noble. It was a nose that meant something, if only you could figure out what.

His eyes were small and narrow, and heavy lidded, giving the impression that he'd just woken up or been born. His hair hung barely to his chin, gold-blond on the surface and velvety dark—nearly black—underneath, when you ran your fingers through it. Obviously I had never run my fingers through Max's hair. But I'm not going to lie and say I hadn't considered it, more than once, more than twice, since the day we'd first met him in the parking garage.

"We got you a present," Francie said to Max. It was news to me. But somehow, there on the edge of the fountain, Francie reached into a gap of air in front of her and plucked out a Swiss Army knife. She held it out to him with a sphinxy gleam in her eyes, a certain mischievousness in her smile. It was a gift; it was a challenge.

Max took the knife from her with dubious curiosity and rolled it over a couple of times in his fingers. He flipped out the blade with his thumb and brandished it in front of his face, let it catch the light. "What did I do to deserve this?" he asked.

"I stole it from Brookstone," Francie said. "I had a feeling we'd see you again, and it seemed like something you would like."

I wanted to know where Francie had gotten that knife. I wanted to know if she had really stolen it with Max in mind. I wanted to know why she had not told me about it.

"Thanks," Max said. "This is awesome. Let's kill someone!" He laughed at his own joke and waved the knife around some more before adding, "Just kidding," although obviously we knew he was kidding.

"Wanna go to the food court?" she asked, even though

she had finished a Cinnabon about five seconds before he had showed up.

"Sure," Max said. I realized suddenly that I had only said one word to him, and that that word had been *hey*. But I didn't know what else to say. I felt like my presence was pretty much beside the point anyway. We took off for the food court, Francie and Max walking together a few paces ahead of me.

"Want to hear a joke?" I heard Francie say.

"Sure," said Max.

"So there are these two blondes in the parking lot," Francie said.

"Okay . . ." Max said. There was a note of uncertainty in his voice, like he was trying to see where she was headed. Like he suspected it was nowhere good.

Francie soldiered on. "So these two bimbos are standing there, trying to unlock the car door with a coat hanger." She paused for effect, to no effect. "And they're, like, fiddling with the door, and it's taking forever, and it's starting to get, like, totally cloudy, and the one blonde says to the other, 'Hurry up, it's about to rain and the top is down!'"

Crickets. Max tilted his head like he was waiting for her to finish, but if Francie noticed that no one was laughing, she didn't betray any discomfort. Francie was really the worst at telling jokes, which was ironic, because she was the only person I knew who enjoyed them. She chuckled to herself and tossed her blond, blond hair. I noticed then that she had just redone it. The roots were mostly gone and it was a slightly different shade than before. Still white-blond, but with a new note of gold somewhere underneath it all. Max turned, looked over his shoulder at me, and raised his eyebrows, smiling. A couple of his teeth were slightly discolored from where I could tell he'd once had braces, his left canine tooth was a tiny bit undersized, leaving a gap. A dimple in one cheek. Max's smile was nearly a snarl, just the right side of vulnerable. All over the mall, you could hear cash registers turning over, *ka-ching*.

"Your friend is crazy," he said to me. "A blonde who tells blonde jokes."

"Crazy!" Francie exclaimed. "Me, crazy! That's a laugh!" She slapped him on the butt, all playful, and skipped ahead a couple of steps. Max looked at me again, shrugged, and this time just mouthed the word. *Crazy*, he said without making a noise.

"Smoothie time!" Francie announced. She took Max's hand and pulled him with her into the food court. It was like the first line of one of Francie's jokes. "A blonde and a brunette meet the world's hottest boy in a parking garage." You could already see how it would all go down.

Chapter Twelve

Francie and I were standing on the escalator, heading down, when she grabbed me by the shoulder. "Look!" she hissed, and gestured across the atrium to a gray-haired woman in a long denim skirt, a purple T-shirt, and a purple felt beret. The woman was wandering through the crowd, pausing here and there to browse shop windows.

"No way," I said. There was no mistaking who it was: our Physics teacher, Ms. Tinker. Francie squealed and applauded silently to herself, then clapped an open hand to her mouth.

"Let's follow her!" she whispered.

"I can't believe she wears that beret even in public," I said. "Does she ever take it off?"

"I bet it smells like cheese. And I bet you a dollar she's gonna go to Ann Taylor Loft and not even buy anything."

"Sucker's bet," I said. "No deal."

Francie swung onto the black rubber escalator railing and vaulted herself across the metal plate onto marble tiles, landing with a triumphant thwack. "Come on," she said. "We can't lose her."

We were in no danger of losing her. If you want to make sure you never get lost in a crowd, a purple beret is really the way to go. Ms. Tinker had just moved from one store to the next; she was outside Crate&Barrel, contemplating a display of flatware.

"Look inconspicuous," Francie said. So we both became our most inconspicuous selves and made our way across the mall to near where our teacher was standing. We lingered behind a ficus, peering through the leaves. Ms. Tinker didn't notice us. She stepped away from the window and started wandering again. Francie took my hand and we moved with her.

It was a little sad seeing our teacher outside of school. She was dressed as if for class, in her *PHYSICS IS PHUN!* T-shirt, her gym whistle dangling familiarly from the lanyard around her neck, the *SAVE THE WHALES* totebag at her side. But here at the mall, shuffling along, Ms. Tinker was different. She had no power over anything at all. She was pathetic, really.

"God, I hate her," Francie said. "She made me and Sandy

come in for a so-called conference last semester—those tardies I told you about. It was a complete joke. She kept calling me *Fanny*."

I giggled. "It suits you," I said.

"Whatever," Francie snorted. "Like it matters if I miss the first ten minutes of Physics? All she's doing is telling us how to label our dividers!"

"She used to teach Special Ed," I told her. "She told us that on the first day, before you showed up. That's why she's so into dividers."

Francie gave me a head shake and otherwise ignored my defense.

Meanwhile, Ms. Tinker was winding her way through the mall, moving with quick and deliberate steps but no clear destination. She was circling and spiraling. Not once did she look over her shoulder. When we passed Crate&Barrel for the third time, Ms. Tinker stopped again to peruse the window display, and Francie turned to me with wide eyes. "This is crazy," she said.

"I know," I said. We could both see what Ms. Tinker was doing, but didn't quite believe it. "She knows the angles."

Francie breathed a low and nearly silent whistle.

And then, just as Francie had predicted, we were at Ann Taylor Loft. Ten paces ahead of us, Ms. Tinker paused at the entranceway, glanced up and down, and adjusted her beret to a suitably jaunty angle. Francie nudged me *I told you so*, but didn't say anything. We just followed her and saw her standing at a rack of white blouses that tied in a ribbon at the collar. We watched her from ten feet away, pretending to be searching for a size at a table of slacks.

"Watch," hissed Francie. "Look! Now!" Just as she said it, Ms. Tinker went blurry for a second; she became somehow indistinct. For a second it was hard to tell what I was looking at, but when I focused—I mean, really focused—I saw our teacher take a can opener from the pocket of her skirt, and then she was stuffing one of the shirts she'd been looking at into her totebag.

Francie and I were both staring, and as Ms. Tinker shuffled past us, she made brief but unmistakable eye contact. She still didn't seem to have any idea that either of us was her student, but it was obvious we'd seen what she had done. And what happened next was truly astonishing. She paused at the doorway and turned around and looked straight at us. She tugged at one ear, then the other. She smiled, wiggled her nose, and paused with a friendly, expectant raise of her brow. She was waiting for a response.

I didn't think about what I was doing, I just did it. I returned the Sign, tug, tug, wiggle. Satisfied, Ms. Tinker nodded and trotted out of the store, back into the mall, leaving Francie and me standing there, too shocked to move.

Francie's jaw dropped. "She just . . ."

"She did," I said.

Francie plopped her ass on the table of mom-slacks and

dropped her bag to the floor. She spread her legs and placed her head between her knees, clutching her temples in her palms. Her hair scraped the floor.

She breathed hard.

"Listen," she finally said when she had righted herself. "So I know I told you that the Sign was like this real thing. . . ."

"Yeah?" I said, with a feeling that I knew exactly where she was going.

She turned away. "I made it up," Francie said. "I mean, it's just some dumb thing I made up."

"Oh," I said. Of course, I had known it all along. I mean, I had, hadn't I? I guess that even though I'd always sort of secretly known, I was still disappointed in her. Not because she had lied, but because by admitting it she was breaking her own rule. She was acknowledging the ordinariness of the world. She was acknowledging her own ordinariness.

The way she was sitting there, so uncertain all of a sudden, shoulders slumped, mouth twitching, she looked like just a little girl. It was like she was a Russian doll and had stepped outside herself as someone nearly the same except smaller, and then again, and smaller, and finally one more time so small that she was hardly there at all. But then she was standing, and as she stood she gathered herself back together, and by the time she was to her feet she was whole again, had collected up every bit of the doubt she'd just betrayed, had hidden it away somewhere where she wouldn't have to think about it. She ran her fingers through her hair, straight down to the ends, and was the same as ever. "Well," she said. "I guess it was real after all. I mean, she obviously knew about it. So that proves it. I guess I'm smarter than I even realized. Just divine inspiration, I guess. I don't believe in God, but I *am* spiritual, you know."

"Exactly," I said. I sort of wasn't a bit surprised. Francie may have thought she had invented the Sign herself, but leave it to Francie to stumble onto something that seemed fake but was in fact 100 percent for real. Leave it to Francie to will something into realness without realizing or even really wanting it. To be accidentally truthful even in the baldest of lies.

Naturally Francie wasn't considering anything like that. It had been completely uncharacteristic of her to doubt herself in the first place—a rare and momentary lapse, and it was already forgotten. Now she had moved on, as she always would, to the greater implications. She was applying a coat of eyeliner, deep in thought. "But Ms. Tinker!" she said to herself. "How can she of all people know? She's our enemy! Our sworn enemy!"

"Maybe not anymore," I said. "She's one of us."

"This ruins everything," Francie moaned. "Ms. Tinker! Can you even imagine? We're ruined!"

"Don't be so sure," I told her. As much as I hated Ms. Tinker, the revelation about our teacher thrilled me as much as it had upset Francie. In a way, it reminded me of the dream I was always having—the one about the mall. A trapdoor you'd never noticed opens. It leads you to the hidden world you always knew was there.

Francie was still reeling and needed to put herself back on an even keel. Nothing made her feel more sure of herself than a shoplifting spree. We headed to Sephora.

And I don't know how it happened. I was doing everything right. Maybe I had gotten cocky. Maybe we were just out of control. We had been stealing more and more, breaking records every day. Or. Maybe I was testing Francie without realizing it. Earlier that day, I'd caught a small glimpse of a different side of her. A Francie who was just a regular girl; a Francie who was powerless. Was that the real Francie? She had lied about the Sign. What else had she lied about? These were important questions.

I was alone in the Stila aisle with a fistful of lip liner when Francie found me. She grabbed my hips from behind and whispered in my ear urgently. "We're caught," she breathed. I couldn't see her, but a tendril of her yellow hair was curling around my shoulder. "Give me your purse," she said, "and get the hell out of here."

I didn't turn around, just shrugged my left shoulder, letting my bag slip into her open palm.

"I can't leave you," I said, still without looking at her.

"Move," she said. "You know the drill. Twenty-five minutes." I was gone.

Francie and I'd had an escape plan worked out since

we'd started at Montgomery Shoppingtowne months ago. Francie had drawn it up and presented it to me in her bedroom, wearing her black-framed glasses for that look of authority, a cigarette tucked behind her ear. She'd made a map and everything and had used a pilfered laser pointer to indicate a route. The plan was this: split up, run for our lives, and meet up at the bus stop by the Burger King, a quarter of a mile away.

At Sephora, though, Francie wasn't following the plan. She wasn't running. As I booked it for the door, I looked over my shoulder and saw her standing there, by herself, my bag in her hand. Lips pursed into stubborn resignation. She was going to take the rap.

I wasn't brave like that. When the guard tried to stop me at the door, I just pushed past him. Everyone knows these mall security guards are just a step up from thieves themselves. Half a step. It's not like they're cops.

"Miss," the guard said, trying to block me with an arm. "You need to come with me."

"Sorry," I spat. And I ran. No one tried to follow. I powered down the phony mall boulevard, up the escalator, and through Macy's, pushing through a crowd of sluggish shoppers. The few times I glanced behind me, the place was deserted, a ghost town.

When I made it to the bus stop, I checked the time every five minutes and watched the horizon, shivering in my parka and awaiting the sight of Francie's blond, shattered halo flying down the sidewalk. It took twenty-five minutes, like she'd said. I'm not proud to say it, but if she hadn't shown at that exact moment, I would have gone home by myself. I wasn't really expecting her. We'd hit Best Buy earlier in the day as well, and between both stores and the two of us, we had easily more than five hundred dollars' worth of stuff.

But Francie surprised me. I should have had more faith in her. I had never doubted her before. She had said she would protect me, and she had.

"Did I miss the bus?" Francie asked when she finally made it. She was hunching, out of breath, still unsteady on her heels.

"Two," I told her. "But you're still right on time. Twenty-five minutes."

"Well, that's something, at least," she said, handing me my purse. I glanced inside and was surprised to see that everything I'd stolen was still in it.

"How did you get out of there?" I wanted to know. "They didn't even take the stuff back?"

"I have my ways," she told me. "I wasn't going to give that shit up; that's some serious makeup. We just need to avoid that particular store for a little while."

"I shouldn't have left you," I said.

"I couldn't let you get in trouble, babe," she laughed, swinging her hair and hitting me on the butt with her purse. "You are too good for words." Then the bus was there.

I should have been grateful, I know. And I was. How could I not be? But I couldn't help wondering: What had Francie done?

You take a seashell. You take a tube of lip gloss and a prissy silk scarf like an English teacher would wear. You take a mountain, and a cloud, and a molten pebble from the core of the world. Francie said this was how we were going to do it. Because the entire planet Earth is pretty fucking big. Francie Knight was big enough to fit it all in her pocket. And climbing onto the J-12 I knew something else about her: she really meant everything she said. It was no exaggeration. Earlier that day, in Ann Taylor Loft, I had come closer than ever to doubting her. But now I knew for sure: she was capable of anything. If she hadn't been before, she was now.

It scared me. The lengths I imagined she might go to. Lengths without limits. But I had already traveled too far with her. And I was not just in it for myself anymore, either. Now there was Jesse to think about. He needed us.

No. He didn't need me. He needed Francie. I hated to admit it, but if I had learned anything that day, it was that I would not be strong enough without her.

Chapter Thirteen

Sleepovers at Francie's house were usually pretty fun, because Sandy tended to be occupied with her internet karaoke habit and really let us do whatever we wanted. As fun as it usually was—the two of us staying up all night with the run of the house—it sometimes made me worry that things could spin out of control. Like, the later it got, the more we risked turning into monsters: by three or four in the morning, Francie and I would both be red-eyed and awake as ever, all wired on Diet Coke and Cheetos, and anything at all could happen. Even something terrible.

One time, in February, I slept over at Francie's. She made me watch this horrible movie that she was really into called *Blue Velvet*. Basically it's about two teenagers who find a severed ear behind the high school and decide to investigate. It really didn't make a lot of sense, but it still freaked me out. Every time I tried to get Francie to turn it off, she would tell me that the best part was coming up, and then the so-called "best part" would be like ten times more fucked up than the last. When the whole thing was over, I told Francie I felt like I'd never be able to look another human being in the eye again.

She just laughed and called me a pussy, and we went up to her room, where she sat me on a stool in front of her vanity and turned on Bronski Beat. She had shoplifted the CD just that day, and I watched her in the mirror as she bopped around to "Smalltown Boy" before finally settling at my back, where she framed my face with her hands and appraised me in the mirror.

"I'm going to give you a makeover," she said. Francie herself was wearing no makeup that night, which was unusual for her, almost without precedent. She considered liquid eyeliner—applied heavily and so frequently that she had to steal a new tube every week or so—to be an essential component of her character. She swore that without it she would lose her mojo. But it was the weekend, and when she came out of the shower, in her pajamas, her face had been scrubbed clean.

"A makeover," I said. I wasn't so sure about it. My hair was growing out a little but was still on the short side, messy, and looked pretty awesome. I kind of liked myself the way I was these days. On the other hand, this was a sleepover, and makeovers were what you were supposed to do. I figured I could humor her. Why not?

At the vanity, Francie stood behind me. "Close your eyes, but don't scrunch," she said. "Relax." I felt her fingertips grazing my cheekbones.

She slathered on the liquid eyeliner until my eyes were Egyptian. She lined my lips in deep red and frosted them whitish pink. A touch of blue powder at my cheekbones. "It's very editorial," she mused. I didn't really know what she meant by that. But when I looked at myself in the mirror, I saw a different person looking back at me. The bloodred lips and death eyes. A corpse's complexion. I saw a vampire: not Samson but Delilah. I couldn't look away. I was so busy staring at myself that I didn't even notice that Francie was leaning in close until I felt her breath in my ear.

"Boo," she whispered.

I screamed. I fell off the stool and onto the floor. "Fuck you," I said. "Are you trying to freak me out?" Francie was laughing too hard to reply—I mean, practically gasping for breath—but she was suddenly interrupted by another scream. It was a scream much louder than mine had been, from somewhere else in the house. A scream like someone was being killed. Then there was a crash.

I looked up at Francie from where I was still lying on the floor. I was terrified for real now, as if I hadn't been totally spooked already. Of course, Francie wasn't even startled. She just stopped laughing, gathered herself together, and smoothed a tired hand through her hair.

"Oh, for fuck's sake," she sighed. "It's just Sandy. Stay here, I'll be back in a second. She gets like this, you know. So crazy."

I was surprised that Francie could be so blasé about a scream like that, but I certainly wasn't about to check it out with her. So I waited. Francie marched off and I pulled my leather notebook out of my bag. I sat at the vanity and began listing the spoils of that day, just to distract myself:

Striped T-shirt, American Eagle, $14.99
Vanilla Spice Shimmer Lip Balm, the Body Shop, $6.00

When I was done listing the spoils of the day, Francie still hadn't come back. I listened, but I didn't hear anything. That big old house felt haunted.

I wasn't afraid of ghosts, but in some ways, at this late hour, Francie and Sandy were more ghostly than the real imaginary thing. And so was I. When I caught a glimpse of myself in the mirror, I was afraid the girl on the other side was going to bust through and kill me and take my place. Where had Francie gone, anyway? I couldn't wait anymore.

So I got up and tiptoed down the dark hall. It was a dark and stormy night, and the floorboards creaked under my feet. I walked past Sandy's bedroom to the wide, twisting stair-case, and peered down over the edge from above. There they were. Francie and Sandy were climbing the stairs together, the two of them illuminated only by the bluish light of a streetlamp through a window, and Francie had an arm around Sandy's waist and another on her shoulder. Sandy was hunched over, stumbling, and muttering something I couldn't quite make out.

"Come on, Mom," Francie said. She hadn't noticed me.

Francie looked different. She looked tired and lonely. Her eyes were flush against the scrunched-up lines of her forehead as she tried to pull Sandy along with her. Sandy wasn't cooperating. "Who do you think you are?" Sandy was saying. "I'm your mother. I'm your mother."

"I know, Mom," Francie said. In that weird light, in boxer shorts and a T-shirt, and without any makeup, even eyeliner, she was almost transparent.

Then she saw me.

She didn't say anything, she just looked at me, and in that moment Francie changed. First a look of confusion, and then rage. And then she was the sun. Just blazing, I'm telling you. She was a ravenous, burning thing. She was on fire.

"Francie," Sandy groaned.

Francie didn't move. She just stared at me. I met her gaze, but only for a second. This Francie was not my friend. I'd never seen her look so angry. This Francie hated me. I turned and ran.

I turned and ran down the long, wide hallway, the kind of hallway that houses don't have anymore, back to her room, where I fell into her bed and just lay waiting.

When Francie returned, she was normal again. It had never happened. "Sorry about that," she said. "Mom had a little too much to drink." But as soon as she said it out loud, I had the feeling it wasn't quite the truth. I wondered why she would lie when she had never been embarrassed about anything before.

"Let's play MASH," she said. She was acting like everything was totally normal. Generally I wasn't into MASH, but it was occasionally fun with Francie, who made up ridiculous categories like Cause of Death and First STD. It was an improvement to the game even if neither of us could ever remember how to spell *chlamydia*. So I sat next to her on her bed and rested my head on her shoulder as she lit a cigarette and drew up the game board.

"I'm sorry," I told Francie as she was ticking off potential futures in her purple spiral-bound notebook.

"Sorry for what?" she asked. The muscles in her neck tensed.

"Never mind," I said. I took a swig of Diet Coke straight from the two-liter bottle. It was going flat and tasted metallic.

"Well, at least you won't be driving a jalopy." Francie crossed *jalopy* off the list of potential vehicles and continued on. Bronski Beat was still on the stereo, and I think we drifted off to the pulse of old-school synthesizers, Jimmy Somerville crooning in that pinched, womanly growl, and

Francie's arm around my shoulder.

That night, when it was almost morning, I killed her. It wasn't me that did it. It was the girl from the other side of the mirror, the one whose lips were icy white and ringed with blood. I stepped outside the mirror when Francie was asleep and took a Mardi Gras necklace from around my own neck. Francie didn't resist as I pulled it tight around her windpipe, twisting and twisting to tighten it, until I couldn't twist anymore. She woke up; her eyes flipped open with a look of inevitability. She knew it had been coming all along. Francie just dropped, and as she crumpled, the necklace snapped, the beads scattering across the floor in a shower of sparkling plastic. Of course, it never happened. But it seemed like it did.

The next morning I woke early, feeling beyond crappy. I had slept only for a few hours. Francie was lying next to me, on top of the covers, breathing and alive as ever. A peaceful look on her face and an unknown word on her lips. Those Mardi Gras beads were still all over the floor. And as hard as I tried, I couldn't sort out the events of the night before. I couldn't remember what was real and what was a dream.

I had to leave. I got up without waking Francie and tiptoed down the stairs, remembering the way Francie had looked at me the night before when she'd held her mother to keep her from falling. That part had happened for real, for sure. On the way down those same stairs, I almost tripped and fell myself, but I caught the banister just in time.

Chapter Fourteen

Around here, there is a creek that touches everyone. It is in every backyard. If you follow the creek in any direction, making sure to keep at least one foot in the water at all times, you will cross deserts, highways, and mountains, but you will always, always reach an ocean.

Around here, there is also a subway. The subway is underneath every backyard. If you are brave enough, you can cross that threshold of earth into some underground, and find a city.

Around here, the suburbs are where you are standing. Somewhere, you know, there is an ocean. You have heard about a city, too, but it is mostly a suspicion. On that Sunday morning in February, the morning after my sleepover at Francie's, the sky was smudged-newsprint white, and I stepped outside the house on Maple, alone, in my black motorcycle jacket and knee-high leather boots, and I was brave. Francie and Sandy were both still asleep. I knew I had to leave them. I wasn't sure where I was going.

The city was only twenty minutes away by train, and the subway stop was right there, but it had never occurred to me, until that morning, to head in by myself. I can't say it was a conscious decision—at the time it just seemed like the path of least resistance. Where else was there to go? I didn't feel like going home, and the mall suddenly seemed like the farthest-away place. So I got on the train.

That morning, the train was filled with strangers who shouldn't have been up in the first place, and I left my sunglasses on so no one could see me staring at them. Across from where I sat, a bum lay across four seats, snoring loudly, drool dripping from his mouth onto the plastic seat and then onto the dirty floor in one long, slimy string. The lights overhead flickered as we left the suburbs, and it wasn't until they came back on that I started to wonder where I was going, and why. It wasn't until the lights came back on that I thought of Francie, on the stairs with her mother. I had stumbled upon something that I was not supposed to know about. Francie had dark secrets.

The trip to the Bahamas. The rumors I'd heard. Showing up out of nowhere. Those long weekends away from home.

My brother standing on the doorstep, duffel bag in hand. Francie in her boxer shorts climbing the stairs. Jesse gone to New York for two years with barely a good-bye. Without thinking about it much, I stepped off the train at a random stop, then looked up and read the pylon above me and realized exactly what I had done. Without even knowing it, I had set myself on a path for Jesse's apartment. Francie had been leading me here: if I squinted, I could see her darting ahead of me, cutting through the crowd, not looking back, just expecting me to follow. Her little black purse had come unfastened, and all her secrets spilled from it, leaving a trail for me. This was her doing.

But it was not Francie's doing. I was alone, and Francie was still in her bed, still asleep, probably dreaming of lip gloss. I had led myself here, on my own impulses. I had kept my fingers pressed to a wall, and now here I was, in my brother's city. I didn't really know where he lived; I'd only been to his place once, years and years ago, but I figured the geography would come to me. I had taken myself this far.

Aboveground, on the street, things were moving. The weather had changed; the sun was out, and it wasn't warm but maybe warm*ish*. Even though the sidewalks weren't crowded yet, the people who were awake looked content and purposeful. Women in chic black, clutching the shoulder straps of their handbags as they made their long strides down the avenue, handsome men ambling along, everyone in and out of restaurants. Dogs on leashes, the smell of coffee. That morning, the street had been flung wide open, and I glanced in all directions until my eye landed on a giant, double-tiered fountain in the middle of a plaza. With no real idea of where else to go, I headed there. There's always something about the fountain, right?

I knew I was on my way to my brother's house, wherever that was, but I wasn't in a hurry. Since it was still winter, the fountain wasn't running, but it didn't matter. I perched on the edge and fingered a pebble in the basin and looked out over the city. When a couple of guys wandered past me with a tiny dog, I asked them for a cigarette and they gave me one, and I sat there, smoking it happily, pleased to be by myself. Suddenly I was in a good mood. When I was done, I went on my way and was trotting down the block when I realized I hadn't brought anything for Jesse.

It was important. I couldn't show up at Jesse's place empty-handed. It barely mattered what I brought him, but I had to bring him something. It had to be stolen. A gift that is stolen can bring a person back to life. So when I passed a dingy liquor store, I ducked inside and headed straight for the counter, where I distracted the clerk with stupid conversation while stuffing my purse with those minibottles of booze. Back on the sidewalk, I was laden with bottles, and I closed my eyes and stared straight up into a cloud until I could feel my pupils as pinpricks.

The last time I had been to Jesse's apartment had been years ago, with my mother, right after he'd moved in the first time. We'd brought him a bouquet of flowers as a housewarming gift, which was foolish, because who brings a man a bouquet of flowers? If you knew my brother you would know a bouquet of flowers was not just foolish but extra foolish, because he's the type of person who, not owning a vase, would have to make do with some makeshift solution like an empty bottle of vodka or something, which is exactly what ended up happening.

I remembered only the most pointless details about Jesse's place. Things like the naked-lady clock he had next to the refrigerator, the contradictory smell of the stairwell— a cross between pee and fancy cologne. Things like the optimism in his voice the day that my mom and I had visited. He'd seemed so hopeful, for that one day, even though we'd just brought him those crappy, useless flowers. I still remembered that. He acted like it was the nicest thing anyone had ever done for him.

I had been wandering aimlessly, and then I was at my destination. I'd known I would find it if I didn't stress too much, and then there it was, on the corner of a side street, right above a small convenience store. I'm not sure how I recognized it, but as soon as I saw it, it all came back to me. This was it, for sure.

Jesse had left home for good the day after high school had ended. He had graduated by the skin of his teeth, and his efforts at the whole college thing had been lackadaisical at best. He'd landed this apartment, taken some classes here and there, waiting tables at night, before finally switching to bartending at some point, and dispensing with the classes altogether. A couple of years ago, he'd sublet the place, and picked up to move to New York. We hadn't heard a lot from him after that, until now. Now he was back.

From the outside, Jesse's building was pretty shitty and falling apart, but it still had a certain ramshackle dignity. You could tell that it had once been nice—fancy, even. Looking up at it—at the cracked stone moldings around the windows and the filthy, elaborate cornices—I imagined Jesse and Liz playing MASH, back in high school, and wondered if this had been predicted for him.

I rang the buzzer. When there was no answer, I rang it again and then again, until I finally heard Jesse's crackling voice, hoarse and scratchy, through the intercom: "Who is it?"

"It's Val," I said. "Your sister."

The door vibrated, startling me, and I pushed it open and ran up the narrow, fouled staircase to the third floor, where Jesse stood in the doorway, in sweatpants and an old T-shirt, eyes puffy and hair matted. "This is a surprise," he said. He seemed a little insane, like everything he said should have been punctuated with an exclamation point. But it was early in the morning.

"Hey," I said. "Sorry to, like, wake you up or whatever."

"No worries," Jesse said. "No worries. I've been awake, actually. But the place is kind of, like, a total dump. You know how it is."

We stepped inside. He was right. It was a complete

dump. Honestly, I wouldn't have expected anything else from Jesse, who had always been an utter slob. The place was tiny and littered with empty cigarette boxes and coffee containers, clothes strewn on every possible surface, and it stank with a gross stench that I couldn't identify. "Let me get some air in here," Jesse said. He flung open a window and cleared a spot for me on an ancient futon by scooping the clothes onto the floor, then plopped himself onto a wooden stool. "So what's up?"

I didn't know how to answer the question. Jesse was fidgeting, running his hands through his hair and drumming his fingers on an end table. He didn't look great. His face was pulled and lined, and his lips were chapped and cracking. It looked like he had been picking at his face.

"I brought you something," I said. And I dumped my purse out onto the couch, spilling forth the small mountain of bottles I'd lifted: Grey Goose and Jack Daniel's and Tanqueray and the rest. Jesse's eyes looked like they were about to pop out.

"No way," he said. "This is too much." And just like that, he seemed better again. "Want a cocktail?" he asked, standing and scooping a couple of the bottles up. "I know it's early, but I'll make something breakfasty."

"Sure," I said.

"So what brings you here, anyway?" he asked from the kitchen alcove, where he was pouring and mixing, humming away like he was suddenly the happiest person on earth.

"I just wanted to see you," I said.

"You never wanted to see me before?" He raised a pointed eyebrow in my direction.

"Oh, like you're one to talk," I said. "Like you're always popping by just to say what's up."

"You got me," Jesse said. "Here." He handed me something pinkish in a martini glass. "Tell me if you like it."

I took a sip. It didn't even taste like booze. It tasted like Crystal Light. "You're a genius," I said.

Jesse sat on the futon next to me and took a sip of his own. He reached over and flicked my ear like he was twelve. "Nah, just been bartending too long," he replied. "I mean, way too long." He sighed. "Man, I need to figure some shit out."

I would never understand my brother. He had been around so much longer than I had, and in the time before my arrival, I knew that he had seen things that had changed him in terrible ways. We had never talked about what, exactly, those things were, but you could tell it all from the way he sometimes tilted his chin and scrunched his mouth to one side of his face: an unconscious wince at some precise angle of injury. The way the muscles in his neck were always clenching and unclenching, then clenching again. I had noticed something in the way Liz had put her hand on his shoulder that night in the basement on Christmas break: like she was trying to bind him, pointlessly, to an Earth that he no longer felt he belonged to.

Jesse wanted to leave. He had one foot out the door. It had been that way as long as I could remember, but I guess he'd always been too much of a slacker to devise a proper exit route. Surely he would figure it out eventually. I don't know—maybe if he looked long enough he would stumble across the schematics to a spaceship, or an interdimensional teleportation device, or a flying car. I'd heard of crazier things. And I guess I thought that if we brought him enough crap, maybe we could weigh him down. Just saddle him up with more and more junk until he was too heavy to break the stratosphere.

"How's Francie?" he asked. "You should've brought her with you. That girl is, like, a trip."

"I didn't feel like it," I said.

"Ah," Jesse said. "Well, that's cool, too. Is everything okay with her?"

"I don't know," I said. "Maybe? I mean, I guess?"

"I get it," he said.

Even though I'd only had a couple sips, the drink Jesse had made me was strong, and I was feeling sort of buzzed. I sat there on the futon staring out the window at the tiny sliver of sky that was visible between two adjacent buildings, and thought that it reminded me of Max for no real reason. I was surprised to be thinking of him; he had snuck up on me. It was like he was so skinny that he was able to slide into the smallest gaps in my thoughts. He was so opposite Francie, who was also skinny but took up so much space.

"It's just that she's different than I expected her to be," I told Jesse. "Well, I mean, it's like she's the same, but it's *things* that are different."

"Maybe you're different, too."

"No," I said, considering it. "Actually, I think I am exactly what Francie expected."

"That's not really what I meant," Jesse said.

"Oh."

"Come stand out on the fire escape," Jesse said. He lifted the screen and crawled over the old-fashioned radiator, out the window, onto the rickety steel balcony outside. I followed him. Out on the fire escape, Jesse perched on the metal stairs, knees wedged in his armpits, and lit a cigarette. "I'm trying not to smoke inside anymore," he said. "It makes everything smell so gross."

I thought it probably wouldn't make much of a difference, but I didn't say anything. "Let me have one," I said. Jesse handed me a cigarette, and stood next to me, arm around my shoulder. His arm felt lighter than I thought it should have. We stood there, barely eleven o'clock in the morning, pink cocktails in hand, shivering a little and staring up at the cold winter sun overhead. So this was the city.

"So are you and Francie, like, in a fight, or what?" he asked.

"No," I said. "It's nothing like that."

"Really. Why are you here then?" he asked. "Obviously

• *136* •

it's nice to have you, but it seems like you're upset or something."

Why had I come here? There was no way I could explain
to him all the reasons, especially since I wasn't exactly sure
of those reasons myself.

"I don't really want to talk about it," I finally said.

"That's fine," Jesse said.

This was his city. He had come here, years ago, I guess
thinking that it would somehow be different. Like it would
transform him. But on the fire escape, above an alleyway, I
could see that it was not different at all. If I was wearing
glasses, I thought, I might be able to see our creek.

"Where were you?" I finally asked him.

"When?" he asked.

"When. I don't know. Anytime."

"Let's just say . . . elsewhere," he said.

"Was Elsewhere any different?"

"No," he said. "It was just the same."

I didn't know what to say to that, so I didn't say anything. I tossed my cigarette over the fire escape and watched
it fall.

"You feel better now, though, right? I mean, every time I
see you it's like you get a little better. Steady improvement?"

From the way he avoided my question, I had the answer
to the question that I had come to investigate.

"Remember that time you and Mom came to visit me
here?" he asked. "Right after I moved in?"

"Yes," I said.

"Things seemed so different then."

"I know," I said. "I mean, I was really little. I was kind of too little to understand what was going on. But things did seem different."

"I always thought you understood everything," he said. "Even when you were practically a baby. You always seemed like you just sort of knew the score better than anyone."

I just looked at him like *Are you insane?* and he shrugged back all, *Well, maybe I am, but still,* and actually, he was right. I did know the score, sort of: he had believed in this city, and in this shitty apartment. He had believed in it, and it had failed him.

"I don't want you to die," I said. "Can you please not die?"

"I'm not going to die," he said. "I'm only twenty-four, you know. Not like I'm some old man or something." But I knew what he really meant to say: *I am barely here now. You won't even miss me when I'm gone. I'm as good as a ghost.*

When I got home, around two, Francie was sitting on my doorstep smoking.

"Hey, bitch," she said.

"Hey, bitch," I said.

"Where did you go?" she asked.

"Elsewhere," I told her. And then, gay as it may be, I just started crying.

Francie kind of melted. "Hey," she said. She stood and put her arms around me and it didn't even feel awkward or anything. I buried my face in the crook of her neck and she mussed my hair. "Don't worry about it," she murmured. "Not to worry. We'll go to the mall; it'll be all better."

I wanted to believe her, I truly did.

Chapter Fifteen

Francie was eating a taco salad. They had put cheese on it by accident, and she was picking it out with her fingers with a look of pure revulsion. Francie hated cheese more than almost anything else on Earth. Just the smell of it disgusted her; I was surprised she was even capable of touching it without rubber gloves.

"I just don't see the point of stealing all that crap," Max was saying. "Not that I'm, like, morally opposed or anything. It just seems like a lot of trouble for shit you don't want."

"Who says I *don't* want a hand-powered flashlight?" Francie asked. She pulled the latest score from out of her bag. "Look, you just turn this crank and it lights right up. You don't even need any batteries. It will charge your cell phone, too, but you have to get the attachment separate. Even so, who wouldn't want something like this?"

"Do you? Want it, I mean?" Max asked.

"Not really," Francie said. "But you're missing the point."

Max laughed. "You and the *point*. Everything always has a point with you. Have you ever considered the fact that some things are pointless?"

"No," Francie said. "That never crossed my mind."

"Okay, well, in that case, what's the point? I want to know." Max leaned in close, chin on his fist.

"The point." Francie racked her brain and came to a satisfactory answer. "Well, for one thing, it's not for me. It's for Val's brother!" she said. She smiled and batted her eyelashes.

"He's *dying*," I added.

Max snorted. "Just what a dying man needs. A hand-crank flashlight." As soon as the words came out, he stopped, turned to Francie, and tugged at his earlobe. "He's not really dying, is he?"

Francie just rolled her eyes.

"You guys are both so full of shit," Max said.

"You wouldn't understand," Francie said. She shrugged and shot a reproachful glance in my direction. A few minutes later, Liz showed up, on her lunch break, and sat with us for a while, trying to trick Francie into having a bite of cheese.

"It will never happen," Francie said. "If someone put a gun to my head, I might consider—*consider*—a bite of mozzarella. But that's as far as I would go."

"You're telling me if someone put a gun to your head you would not eat a bite of Gouda?" Liz asked.

"I would not," Francie said. "Not even a crumb." She folded her arms across her chest with cheerful intransigence. She was loving the attention. Attention made Francie stronger. If no one gave a shit about her, I figured, she would just cease to exist.

"What about pizza?" Liz was asking.

I had a hard time figuring out why Liz was always hanging out with us. She was so much older—practically a grown-up. But for some reason she was always around now. She had even called me at home one time just to chat. I'd been flattered, but also nervous and unsure of what exactly to say. We'd just sat on the phone for ten minutes, awkward, the conversation punctuated by long bursts of silence. Then I told her I had homework to do.

Liz had started throwing little balls of cheese at Francie, who was screaming and dodging them while these prissy girls at the next table gave us dirty looks. "Fuck you," Liz finally shouted at them, and threw some cheese in their direction. "I'm an *assistant manager!*" she snarled.

"Maybe we should go before we get kicked out," Max suggested.

"They can't kick me out," Liz sighed. "My shift's not over yet. We just got a new shipment, too. Can someone please kill me?"

"Buck up, Liz," Francie said. "Back to work, all of us. We

need to take some more stuff if we're going to make our quota for the day."

Max groaned. "Now you have a quota?"

"I just instituted one," Francie said. "Meet the new boss, same as the old boss."

"Can't we do something that's fun for everyone?" Max asked.

"You don't have to come if you're not feeling it," she replied. "No one's forcing you. Val and I have a calling. It's not our concern that you don't care about anything except that dumb skateboard."

But Max's hard-on for Francie wouldn't allow him to go his own way. He trailed behind us to Express, then hung outside as we stepped in to do our thing.

Express was turning over its merchandise for spring. I took inventory of the clerks in their corners, changing mannequins and unpacking cardboard boxes. My skill inhabited me. Disappearance tingled in my fingers. I twisted the rubber bands at my wrist, ready to pull them tight around sensors, pop them right off. No matter what, the moment before the rip-off would always be exciting—that would never change—but lingering in the entranceway, even with that feeling of anticipation building in the pit of my stomach, I realized there was nothing in the store that I wanted.

Francie's breath was hot in my ear. "Go for the big score," she whispered from over my shoulder. "Today could be the day we finally find it. I've got a good feeling about today. I think Max is good luck."

I took it all in: the candy-colored tanks, the breezy, bias-cut skirts, and skinny jeans, and dressy-casual blouses. It was all crap. And I wasn't trying to be bitchy, I was just calling it as I saw it. "It's not like we're really going to find it at Express," I said. It was just an observation. But it was the first time that I'd ever questioned her aloud like that.

She frowned. "Jeez," she said. "You'll never win with a badditude like that."

"I'm just being realistic."

"Like I said. Bad attitude. Come on. This one's all you. I'll watch your back."

I could feel Max's eyes on us from where he sat on a bench outside the store. I knew the point of focus for every clerk in the store and I could easily pick out the manager just from the shininess of her ponytail, along with the assistant manager from the way she kept glancing at the real manager from the register. "I can watch my own back," I muttered.

Francie pulled back. Her hand flew from its perch on my shoulder blade. "I know you *can*. I was just . . ." She trailed off and sighed. "Never mind. Do your own thing, babe."

So I did my own thing. I watched my own back. It wasn't hard at all.

I didn't score big that day. I could have if I had wanted to. I just didn't feel like it. Instead, I aimed low, stealing two camisole tank tops, one for me and one for Francie. It wasn't the type of thing we would normally wear, but the weather had actually turned nice and I figured we could celebrate by going sleeveless.

"Just a couple of tank tops?" Francie asked when I showed her what I'd taken.

I shrugged. "It's Express," I said. "What do you expect?"

"Well, I get the purple one," she said. "Purple has always been my color." Purple had never been Francie's color. It was just her way of taking control of the situation.

We all decided to walk home instead of taking the bus. It was a couple miles, but the sky was finally blue. Max rattled along on the sidewalk while Francie and I dawdled together at a distance, passing a cigarette back and forth between us. Francie had taken off her heels and they dangled from her fingers. She walked with ginger precision to avoid the broken glass and sharp pebbles on the sidewalk as traffic sped by.

We were both watching Max roll ahead of us on his board, his pants barely hanging on, an inch of boxers poking out from the waistband of his jeans.

"What do you think his deal is?" asked Francie.

"What do you mean?" I asked.

"Well, have you noticed he doesn't have any friends except us? And are we even his friends? I mean, are we really? Consider it."

"You and I don't have any friends except each other, either," I said. "What's the difference?"

"It's different for boys," said Francie. "Everything is

different for boys. The way they travel in packs. The way they hardly seem to care at all about anything. What passes for conversation: *"'Hey, bro,' 'What up, bro,' 'What's goin on, you homo, bro?'"* She gave me a mocking high five and pinched my ass. "There should be, like, five guys skateboarding along with him right now. That's how it normally works. But it's just him. Why do you suppose that is? I've been thinking about it."

I took a drag off her cigarette. "Maybe he doesn't need any friends," I said.

"I don't know. He's not like us," Francie told me. "Not like me, at least, that's for sure. You can tell he used to be normal. You can tell from the way he moves, the way he talks. *'What up, bro, you fuckin' fag?'* I can totally hear it. He used to be like any of the rest of them. Something happened. What happened? Dark secrets. Mark my words, Val."

"If you say so," I sighed. But I didn't really believe her. "What kind of person actually says 'Mark my words,' anyway? Besides a cartoon character?"

Francie raised an evil eyebrow and pressed her fingers together as if contemplating nefarious plans. "Let's see: a robot. A hologram. Mua-ha-ha-ha!" she cackled. And then her face softened. She dug into her purse, whipped out a rubber band, and pulled her hair into a ponytail. "But he is cute, right? I mean, he just is."

"He is," I said. "And he's, like, totally in love with you. I can tell."

"I know," she sighed. "It's sweet. Those puppy-dog eyes. But I don't have time for a boy in my life. I'm too busy with my scheme for world domination. I would never let a boy stand in the way of that, no matter, like, how hot."

"Can't you rule the world *and* have a hot boyfriend?" I asked.

"Not Max," Francie said. "He's the type who's trouble. The type to fuck up even the best plan."

"How do you know that?" I asked. "What are you basing this on?"

"I'm not basing it on anything," Francie said. "It's just what I believe."

"You're always saying that," I said. "Like just the fact that you believe it makes it automatically true."

"Doesn't it?" Francie asked, only half-kidding. "I mean, have my beliefs ever failed us?"

I didn't answer her, just grabbed her hand and swung our arms between us in a wide and sweeping arc.

Francie believed in certain things. It was part of what made her interesting. The things that Francie believed in defined her. But what would happen if one of Francie's so-called *beliefs* turned out to be wrong?

Chapter Sixteen

"Did you hear about the blonde who thought nitrates were cheaper than day rates?" Francie asked. She was lying upside down on her bed with her legs propped up against the wall and her head dangling off the edge. Her hair reached almost to the carpet.

"That's the dumbest one yet," I said, barely paying attention to what she was saying. I was sitting there next to her, scribbling in my notebook. It wasn't that I didn't care about what she was talking about; we were having one of those moments when it was okay to space out. "It doesn't even make sense."

"That's kind of why I like it," Francie said. "I found it on the internet. Now they're telling us we're stupid for not knowing what a nitrate is? What next? Did you hear about the blonde who never made it all the way through *Gravity's Rainbow*?" In one graceful move, she flipped around and was sitting upright, back straight and neck stretched with swan-like poise. She gave me a look of deep inquisition. "What *is* a nitrate, anyway?"

"Something totally gay," I said. It's what she wanted me to say.

"I tried to read *Gravity's Rainbow* over the summer," Francie said. "Personally I thought it was pretty fucking stupid."

Did you hear about the blonde who was treated at the emergency room for a concussion and severe head wounds? She'd tried to commit suicide by hanging herself with a bungee cord. Did you hear about the blonde who tried to blow up her husband's car? She burned her lips on the tailpipe. Did you hear about the blonde whose boyfriend said he loved her? She believed him.

And did you hear the one about the blonde who traveled to the edge of the world and unpacked her suitcase and began throwing everything she owned into the abyss? Did you hear about how her clothes burst into flames when they plummeted into the endlessness, and how she stood there, at the end of everything, naked and watching it all go, and how she wasn't sad about it at all?

Me either. But I wouldn't be surprised if it had happened, once, just like that. If it hasn't, I'm sure it will someday.

There was a knock on Francie's bedroom door. It was Sandy. She walked in and began rustling through Francie's stuff.

"Hi, *Mom*," Francie said. "What are you doing?"

"Can I have a cigarette, dear?" Sandy asked.

Francie reached for the box at the foot of her bed and handed her mother a Misty. "You shouldn't smoke, Sandy," she said. "I read somewhere it makes you grow hair on your palms."

Sandy paid her daughter no mind. She sat down on the floor facing us, and crossed her legs Indian-style. She lit up. Sandy was always trying to hang out with us like this, but it was pretty rare that Francie allowed it, and in general, Sandy followed Francie's many instructions to the letter. Even when it hurt her feelings. If Francie had told her mother to fuck off, Sandy would have smiled a weak, pathetic smile, chuckled like it was all a joke, and retreated instantly, closing the door behind her with barely a click. But Francie was apparently in a charitable mood, and Sandy was beaming at being allowed into the inner sanctum, even briefly.

"What's going on, girls?" Sandy asked. "I feel like I never get to talk to you about your lives."

"Did you hear the one about the blonde who thought a sanitary belt was a drink from a clean glass?" Francie said.

"What's a sanitary belt?" I asked.

"I don't get it at all," Sandy said. "And I'm old enough to know what a sanitary belt is."

"I don't get it, either," Francie said. "I was hoping you could explain."

Sandy was one of the saddest people I had ever encountered, like, ever. Even sadder than my own cocker spaniel of a mother, and that was saying a lot. Sandy had no friends and no life. She stayed up almost all night and woke up at five or six in the morning, but all she ever seemed to do with all that time was drink red wine, order things from QVC and eBay, and devote herself to her online karaoke hobby, for which she had set up a makeshift studio in the basement. Sandy was desperate for attention but incapable of commanding it. She never left the house as far as I knew, except—I guess—for groceries, which they don't sell on late-night cable. Although there was that one trip to the Bahamas. She had to have left the house for that. Otherwise never.

The thing that was hardest to conceive, so to speak, was that Sandy had once had sex with a man in order to produce Francie. She was beautiful; it wasn't that. It was just that I couldn't imagine her ever associating with any person long enough to do it with him. Where would she have even met a guy? I figured she must have been different in those days. This was confirmed by Francie, who had told me that during her own formative years, Sandy had been a total slut, with a string of asshole boyfriends constantly parading through the house. Things had changed.

In Francie's room, Sandy was standing at the window,

wiggling her hips to the Smiths, and snapping the fingers that weren't clutching her cigarette. *"Hand it over/Hand it over/Hand it over."* "I wonder if they have this song on karaoke?" she said. "Val, do you like online karaoke?"

"Um . . ." I said. Sandy was being even weirder than usual. She was swaying faster and faster, completely off the beat. She did a little pirouette across the room and tossed her hair and laughed long and loud and openmouthed.

"Leave us alone, Sandy," Francie said, and her mother nodded and smiled sheepishly and got lost.

It was almost ten o'clock when we discovered that Sandy had disappeared. Actually I was the one who made the discovery. I'd thought it was kind of weird that she wasn't on her usual perch in front of the television as I was leaving, and that I didn't hear any caterwauling from the basement, but it wasn't until I stepped out onto the front stoop that it struck me something could be really wrong. I had stepped out of this door so many times; Francie's yard was so familiar to me that I knew something was off but couldn't quite put my finger on it.

Standing there in the early-spring nighttime, the streetlights buzzing as if telling me to look more closely, I scrutinized the dim landscape of the lawn. There was the maple tree, just starting to win its leaves back. The weathered picket fence with the broken gate. There was the funny pipe sticking up out of the grass next to the azaleas, and there was the driveway. And then it came to me: the Jaguar was gone. The Jag had never not been in the driveway. The Jaguar was always in the driveway. It was like looking at a picture of someone with no eyebrows.

"Hey, Francie!" I shouted, poking my head back inside. But Francie already knew what had happened. She was standing in the middle of the living room, flipping the pillows over on the couch and searching for something.

"Mom?!" she called. But I could tell that she was past the point of expecting an answer. "Fuck! Sandy?! I am going to kill you!"

"Francie," I said. "What's going on?"

She looked at me, and it was the same look I had seen her give me that night on the stairs with her drunk mother draped around her shoulders. This time, although I was still a little bit scared, I stood my ground. I just had a feeling it was the right thing to do. "Francie," I said again. "What's going on?"

"Fuck, fuck, fuck" was all she could say. Without being invited, I stepped back inside. I didn't bother to close the front door. I wanted to do something, but I felt helpless. Francie was flipping out.

"I can't believe she's pulling this crap again," she said. "You should go home."

I folded my arms across my chest. "No," I said. I wasn't sure if Francie was trying to protect me or herself, but either way, I thought I'd earned the right to know certain things.

Francie looked like she was going to argue, but she didn't bother. "Well, then, do something. Get me the phone."

Without knowing what was happening, but understanding the sense of urgency, I ran to the kitchen to get the phone. It felt important to have a task. Francie just snatched it from me when I dashed back and punched a number into the speed dial. She fidgeted with her hair while she waited for the pickup. She wouldn't look at me; she just stared at the ceiling.

"Dan? It's Francie," she finally said. "She did it again."

A pause. Even though she wasn't looking at me, I could see the familiar eye roll from the way her cheeks tensed. "I don't care where you are. I need you. Get over here." And "Asshole," under her breath when she hung up.

At this point, I didn't bother asking her any questions. I didn't try to touch her. I sat on the couch and waited patiently for all to be revealed. She didn't talk to me for a few minutes, just made herself busy with something or other in the kitchen, but then she reappeared with a bottle of wine and beckoned. "Come on," she said. "Dan's coming over. Let's wait outside."

Francie and I sat on the stoop together, each smoking our own cigarette and passing the wine between us. I was afraid to say anything, but finally I couldn't help myself.

"Who's Dan?" I asked. "You never said anything about anyone named Dan before."

Francie sighed and took a deep drag before answering.

"He used to be my mom's boyfriend," she said. "He lived with us for almost a year, but it was a long time ago. He's actually not so bad; he's, like, the closest thing I have to a dad, I guess. Okay, stepdad maybe? Uncle? I don't know. He stuck around longer than anyone else. And . . . you know. He helps out sometimes."

"Sometimes like when?"

"Sometimes like *this*," she said. "Listen, in case you hadn't guessed, my mom is crazy. I mean, really crazy. I mean, totally bonkers." She twirled her finger at her temple as if it was a big joke, and continued. "When this happens, he helps. It's the least he can do. I mean, really, he could do a whole lot more."

"Oh," I said.

Francie tossed her finished Misty onto the lawn and lit another one. "You're going to see some real insanity tonight, believe me," she said.

A few minutes later, a red Pathfinder pulled up and a guy climbed out. It was Dan. He was younger than I expected—maybe midthirties—and kind of hot, too, in a gone-to-seed kind of way. He pulled the broken gate aside and walked up to us in a weary lope. I saw a cheesy tribal tattoo inching out from under the sleeve of his T-shirt.

"Francie, I thought I told you to stop smoking those fucking cigarettes. Do you really want to have lung cancer by the time you're twenty-five?"

"I think if there's a time for smoking, this is it," she retorted, and blew a cloud of smoke right into his face. Dan glared at her. She made a face in return. "Anyway, this is Val."

"Hi," I said.

"Hi," he said. "Put the cigarette out." I did, and he shook my hand.

"Any idea where she went?" he asked Francie.

"I just hope she didn't go to the homeless shelter again. That was ridiculous."

"Tell me about it. I can't believe she thought you were trying to *poison* her."

I was pretty mystified as to what was going on, but I didn't push it. I would find out.

"Want me to drop Val off on the way?" Dan asked.

"I'm coming," I said firmly. He glanced sidelong at me with gentle suspicion.

"Okay," he said. I reached into my purse and shut off my cell phone so my mom wouldn't be able to bug me. We all climbed into the Pathfinder, Francie riding shotgun, and took off.

Heading off into the night, in the back of the truck, I felt as if I was embarking on a great adventure. I felt like we might not be coming back, like we were off on a grand quest; those funny gnomes in *The Lord of the Rings* leaving home for the first time and venturing into the unknown to save the world.

But the mood in the front seat was different. All I could see was the back of Francie's body. From the way she held her head, the way her shoulder was slumped against the window, I could tell that this was no adventure to her. It was a chore, like taking out the trash. Maybe more upsetting, but no less rote. From time to time she and Dan would exchange a fatigued look.

From what I could tell, we were driving just to drive, without any idea where we were going.

"The library's closed," Dan said. "She can't be there."

"The park would be dangerous. Even Sandy wouldn't go to the park at this hour. Would she?"

"God," Dan sighed. "It never changes, does it?"

We were heading into the city, I guess for a lack of any-place else to go. Francie unrolled the window and lit another cigarette, and this time Dan didn't bother to say anything about it. Instead, he flipped the radio on and tuned in one of those soft-rock stations that gives gooey dedications into the night. "I would like to request a song for my beautiful lady," the guy on the radio was saying.

"We should request a song for Sandy," Dan said. "She loves this show. Maybe she would hear and realize we're looking for her. She always seems surprised, like it never would have occurred to her that we would be worried."

Suddenly Francie squealed and tossed her just-lit cig. "I have an idea!" she said, clapping her hands. Her mood instantly changed; nothing cheered Francie like a brilliant scheme. She pulled out her cell phone and her wallet with her emergency credit card. She looked at the back of the card for a moment, returned it to her purse, and dialed a number. "I'd like to report a stolen card," she said. "My name is Sandra Knight. I lost it three or four hours ago. Have there been any charges? No, I don't know the number, but I can give you my Social."

I could practically see Francie's ears twitch as she listened to the person on the other end. She gestured frantically for me to give her something to write on, and I rummaged through my purse and tossed my notebook to the front seat. Francie began to scribble.

"Well, it's official: my mother is crazier than ever," she said when she'd hung up. "This is going to take forever. She's checked into almost every hotel in the city."

"What do you mean?" I asked.

"I mean, she's been going to hotels all night. She goes to one; she checks in; she leaves. She goes to another one; she checks in; she leaves. Et cetera."

"Why would she do that?" I asked.

Dan laughed.

"I told you," Francie said. "Bonkers! Now let's see . . ." She began to read off the list of hotel names.

"Let's start with the Embassy Suites," Dan said. "I think it's closest."

"Why don't we just call?" I said.

"I'm sure she used a fake name," Francie said, handing

my notebook back along with her phone. "But it's worth a try. Try 'Darcy Farcy.' It's one of her favorites."

I started dialing while Dan sighed and cruised down Wisconsin, into the city. There was no Sandra Knight—and no Darcy Farcy—checked in anywhere.

"Ask for 'Dolores Pizza,'" Francie hissed, listening in. "She uses that one sometimes, too." But it was no good.

We got to the hotel and double-parked outside. Dan went to the counter to try to explain the situation while Francie and I checked out the bar. She wasn't there. We went from there to the Sheraton, the Hilton, and the Marriott, all of which she'd made charges at in the last three hours, according to the Visa lady. Still no Sandy. Francie tried to order a martini at the Hilton bar, and the bartender actually laughed in her face.

As the night wore on, Francie's spirits seemed to waver again. We were on the right track, but the possibilities, however narrowed down, still seemed endless. Sometimes you could judge Francie's mood from her hair, and the carefully teased mane she'd started the night with was sinking like a ruined soufflé. "We have to find her," Francie said. "You have no idea what she might do."

"I guess I don't," I said.

But we did find her, eventually. When we finally found Sandy, she was sandwiched between two men at the

Doubletree bar, laughing her head off. She looked up with surprise when she spotted Francie, then beckoned her over. "Francie! What are you doing here? And you too, Val! Do you girls want a drink? Val, I think Greg here might be just your type." She elbowed the chubby, bald old man on her left and winked saucily, making kissy noises. The guy leered at me.

Francie pulled him out of his seat and tossed him aside. "I'll take a Long Island Iced Tea." She plopped down in the newly vacated stool next to her mother and shooed Greg away when he tried to hover. Dan looked disapproving of the drinking, but we didn't leave until Francie had swallowed the last drop.

"Your card's been denied," the bartender said when Sandy went for the tab.

There was a cop car parked outside my house upon our arrival. The sun was almost coming up.

"Shit," I said.

Dan looked at me like I was crazy. "Didn't you tell your parents where you were going?"

I shrugged.

"Why do I do this?" Dan wondered aloud. "I can't believe I'm still doing this crap. Do you want me to come in and explain?"

"No," I said. "I think that might just freak her out even more."

"Valentina's mom loves strange older dudes with tattoos," Francie said.

"Maybe I should talk to her," Sandy said. "I'm reputable, after all!" She winked at me in a just-between-us-girls kind of way and giggled and tossed her hair.

"I'll be fine," I said, and I hopped out of the truck and scrambled up the lawn.

I was grounded, but it didn't matter anyway, because Francie was gone again. At least this time she told me she was leaving for a while. *Off 2 Bahamas again! B back soon!* she'd texted me. *Not funny,* I texted her back.

I spent my time in lockdown in my room listening to music I knew my mom hated and catching up on my homework. I was getting an F in French, having done practically nothing in the class, but my teacher had told me I could still make up the work and maybe pull out a C. *"Être, être, être,"* I wrote. "To be (infinitive). *Je suis, je suis, je suis. Nous sommes, nous sommes, nous sommes. Tu es, tu es, tu es. . . ."* And like that. After a while it started to feel good, just the repetition of it.

It took me a couple of days to finish every last assignment. At first I was at a loss for what to do next, but then I decided to play dress-up. I laid out all my clothes on the floor of my bedroom and surveyed them. I retrieved all the makeup I'd stolen, almost none of which was even opened, from its hiding spot under the bed. "What would Francie wear?" I asked myself.

But that wasn't really the right question to ask. I had been imitating Francie's style since I first met her. And that time in her bedroom, she had given me that makeover and turned me into a bizarre version of herself. It hadn't worked.

"What would Francie *not* wear?" I asked myself instead. I picked out my old baggy mom-jeans and an ugly cable-knit turtleneck sweater from the back of the closet. I put them on and looked at myself in the mirror. My hair was chin-length now, and greasy and lifeless. I looked like I was wearing a costume. It wasn't right. It was not who I was. I'm not sure if it was who I had ever been.

And then I asked myself: What would *I* wear? And I put on my black jeans and my black knee-high boots. I zipped my motorcycle jacket up over bare skin, just high enough so you couldn't see my nipples. I greased my hair back into a slick pompadour.

"What are you wearing?" my mother asked when I went downstairs for a glass of milk.

"It's my new look," I told her. "Do you like it?" It was the same thing I had been wearing since at least December, except usually I wore a shirt under the jacket. I guess she just hadn't noticed before. Or maybe it somehow looked different on me now.

"You look like a witch," my mother said. I made my witchiest face, and she actually laughed.

My mother had been making an effort to be nicer to me since my grounding. I don't know if she felt guilty about it or what. But she had actually been acting like a real person. It was weird.

"When you say this is your new look," she asked, "does this mean you're going to be dressing like this all the time?"

"Yes," I said.

"I Innn," she said, and she nodded impassively.

When I turned around to leave, she added, "I don't care what you wear. I really don't. But don't do that to me again. Having to worry about your brother constantly is about as much as I can possibly handle. I rely on you to be good."

"The good times are over," I said.

Francie returned a week later. My mother had wanted me to be grounded longer, but she didn't have the energy to keep me all locked up and everything. For the first time ever, Francie wasn't in the mood for the mall, so we went for a walk instead. It was a little awkward being around her again; I honestly had no idea what to say. It seemed like she didn't, either. I sort of thought she was actually embarrassed.

We went to the park and strolled together for what seemed like forever, down the winding asphalt bike path, across University Boulevard, farther out than I had ever walked before.

"Well," Francie said, "I guess you figured out I never went to the Bahamas. We never went anywhere at all. I mean, we did, just not the Bahamas. I've never even been to the Bahamas. We did go to Hawaii once when I was little."

"So where were you over Christmas, then?" I asked.

"At my grandma's," Francie said. "My mom went to the hospital. Same as this time. It happens sometimes. She loses it and checks in for a couple of days until the insurance people tell her she has to leave. Of course, she's never totally better; give her three months and it'll be the same old story. This time was actually no big deal, really. Over Christmas she tried to kill me!"

"What?"

Francie nodded furiously with a triumphant grin. "She thought I was the devil!" Francie chirped. "So she came at me with a potato peeler!"

I didn't know what to say to that.

"Oh," I said. "She really tried to kill you?"

"Well, no, but she did wave a potato peeler at me, like an inch from my face. It was so ridic."

"Isn't your grandma concerned about this insane situation?"

"Ha! My grandma is a total bitch. She would make you want to puke. I mean, there's really no question about how my mom turned out so fucked-up in the first place."

"Why didn't you tell me?" I asked her. "Why did you lie? You could have at least told me you were going away. It was so weird."

"A person can have secrets," Francie replied. "It's nothing personal. You have secrets. All those secrets about your brother. And I've barely even *met* your mom."

"You know basically as much about my brother as I do. I hardly know my brother at all. And anyway, it's different," I said.

"How?"

"I don't expect secrets from you because you act like you have none."

Francie and I had traveled out to the edge of the park, and we'd taken our shoes off and had sat down on the rocky bank of the creek, where we dragged our bare toes through dirt and pebbles. I tried to skip some rocks across the surface, but I couldn't quite master the flip of the wrist. They kept sinking.

"What I *act* like has almost nothing to do with the person I actually am," Francie said.

"Pardon me if I say that comes as a surprise," I told her.

All of a sudden, it was spring, and I glanced over at Francie, who was standing and dusting off her ass, and there she was at her most shining. She was untroubled and epic; bigger than her own body. Francie's hair was blonder and longer and wilder than ever, just the way it sometimes looked in my dreams. In fact, she was exactly how I had always imagined her.

But then a cloud passed in front of the sun, and the sky darkened—only a fraction, but still darkened—and spring was gone. Francie was not how I imagined her but how I knew other people saw her. I was only starting to understand that it might be how she saw herself, too.

It made me sad.

"I'm sorry," Francie said. "Things are complicated some-times. I wouldn't expect you to understand."

Francie stood and stripped down to the lacy frillery we'd stolen together, months ago, from Victoria's Secret, and waded into the dirty, slimy, and probably toxic creek until she was in up to her hips. Her teeth started chattering. Despite the warmth in the air, it was still only barely spring. But she fell backward into the water and was totally submerged save for the tangle of hair floating on the surface like a wayward bird's nest.

She stayed under until I thought she might be dead. When she finally emerged from the water, her underwear was see-through and dripping and her hair had turned green. I half expected her to have transformed herself into a sea monster, or a yellow bird that could take off now for another life. But she had not. She just moved toward me, ris-ing with every step.

"Did you hear about the blonde who . . ." she started.

"Yes," I cut her off. "I already heard about her."

Chapter Seventeen

Francie wanted me to come over, but I wasn't in the mood. I walked her back to her place and then headed to the mall by myself.

It had been forever since I'd ridden the J-12 without her. Sitting on the bus alone that day, I felt outside of myself. I was floating; I was looking down over the suburbs with a clear eye. *Here is Sandra Dee Senior High School. Here is my house. Here is the hospital, and the mall, and the creek that touches everything. Like the creek and the mall, I am part of all of this.*

I was perversely angry that Francie wasn't with me. She was a part of everything, too. Even though I'd basically ditched her, I wanted her with me anyway. And when I climbed down onto the sidewalk and looked up at the fortress of the mall, I was filled with—I don't know—like, this infinite longing.

The mall had been good to me. It had brought me Francie. I had thought that would be enough, and for a while it had been. Now I was asking it for something more, but exactly what I wanted, I couldn't start to say. I scrambled over the break in the chain-link fence and climbed the grassy hill into the parking garage, like I'd done so many times before.

The mall had thrown up a wall of fog; I could barely find my way from entrance to atrium. I tried to retrace old paths only to find myself back in the place where I'd started. I was worried that without Francie I wouldn't be able to steal any-more, but when I finally I made it to Bath & Body Works, my gifts were still with me. I took some bath beads, some soap, and some body lotion. It was easy. But it wasn't very satisfying.

Then I was at the edge of the fountain, and Max was there, unexpectedly, waiting for me. Max was one of those people whose only reliable trait was his unreliability. He had only showed because I hadn't been expecting him. He looked hot as ever, in a pair of mangled, loose-fitting jeans and a blue pullover hoodie, his hair messy and kind of greasy, but in a good way. He gave me that odd, winning smile.

"Where's your friend?" he asked.

"She couldn't make it," I told him. Did anyone ever think about anything other than Francie?

"That girl confuses me," he said.

"You confuse her, too," I told him. "She mentioned it the other day."

"She thinks she knows everything."

"I know."

"She's not as smart as she thinks, you realize."

"You'd be surprised."

Max had this way of talking in asides, like nothing he was saying had anything to do with what the conversation was actually about, even if it did. "Why do you like her?" he asked me.

"Francie? What, you don't like her?"

"Of course I like her. I'm just curious why you do."

"I guess it's like . . ." I considered it for a second. "I guess it's that I've never met anyone like her before. Someone who just doesn't care. It's like she was sent here from an alien planet, or the future. A strange visitor. It's like she's here to teach us something."

"What's she supposed to teach us?" Max asked.

"Something important," I said. "Something besides shoplifting. That's all I know. With these strange visitors, it's not supposed to be too obvious. If it was that simple, they would just tell you outright or send it in a postcard or something."

"I guess you're right about that."

"She's my best friend," I said. "She really is. Actually, she's my only friend."

"I'm your friend," Max said. He dipped his hand into

the fountain and splashed some water on my leg. "I've never seen you without her. You look beautiful without her."

"That's a weird thing to say," I said. Max was nothing if not a flatterer. I'd seen him doing it to Francie, too; the difference was that she fell for it. I stood. "Want me to show you how to shoplift?"

"Not really," he said. "Want me to teach you how to skateboard?"

"No."

"Let's just go for a walk, then," Max said.

So we went for a walk. We walked the length of the mall, and then the width, and then the entire perimeter of the wraparound balcony that was the second floor. We talked about a lot of stuff, most of it unmemorable. But even though the stuff we were talking about wasn't important at all, I was happy to be talking to someone other than Francie. I had practically forgotten what it was like to have a conversation with someone else. Francie was all bright eyes and brass tacks, and every time you had a conversation with her, you got the feeling that she was trying a case, that every nonsensical thing she said was all a piece of a mystifying, aggregate thesis. It was kind of exhausting. Max, by contrast, barely seemed to know what was coming out of his mouth as he said it.

"I've got this dog," Max said. He was mumbling like he was embarrassed to hear his own voice, but he just had to say it anyway because it was important.

"A dog. Cool," I said.

"His name's Noodle. Stupid name, I know, but it wasn't my idea, and he's an awesome dog. He's a golden retriever. The best dogs ever."

"I hear they're very loyal."

Max considered his words. "I think it's so shitty when people talk about how dogs are, like, bred to love people, because that makes it seem so much stupider than it is. If something's programmed to love you, or if it just loves you because it doesn't know any better, well, what's the point of that? It's meaningless."

"I've always been kind of afraid of dogs," I said.

"You wouldn't be afraid of my dog," he said. "He's the best. But what I'm saying is, like, if dogs just loved you because that's what dogs do, it would be so empty. It would be like having a robot. Or one of those weird life-size sex dolls that cost five thousand dollars."

"Gross," I said. "Anyway, I thought dogs loved whoever fed them."

"I mean, *true*, but that's missing the point. It's not like dogs love *you*, or *me*, or anyone. It's more like—like they're the living embodiment of everything that is good. Or like they're vessels for it," Max said. "Like when I take Noodle to the park. He's out running in the field, he's chasing whatever, and all you see is this blur of yellow, and then he'll, like, disappear for a minute or two, and then suddenly he'll be right there at my feet, panting, and when he looks up at me, I'll look at him, and it's not that I can see that he loves me. I know he does love me, and I love him, too, but that's not what I see. What I can see is, like, all the love in the entire world. Right there, those black eyes, tongue all wagging. It's practically bursting out of him. This boundless, cosmic *affection*."

"Are you stoned?" I asked.

"Come on," Max said, wounded. "I'm talking about serious shit here."

"No, really. Are you stoned?"

"Only a little bit." He shrugged. "So I smoked a bowl like an hour and a half ago. That doesn't mean I'm not being totally serious."

"The funny thing is that I know what you mean," I told him. "Even though you're stoned and I don't like dogs."

We were facing each other. I looked at him, with his scruffy not-quite-beard, his blondish hair. His eyes were watery and bloodshot, which had the strange effect of making them all the bluer. He had run out of things to say.

"You know, you kind of look like a golden retriever," I told him. "You really do."

"People always say I look like Noodle," he said.

"That's such a stupid name."

"I know," he admitted.

"I'm going to steal something for you," I told him.

He cocked his head at me like he was going to say no, and then he laughed and shrugged, and we walked into Steve & Barry's, where I made an ugly camo hat disappear into my bag.

"This camo shit is so finished," he said when we were outside and I placed the hat on his head. But he looked pleased that I'd actually stolen it for him, and he flipped the brim a little, giving him a boyish aspect, like Dennis the Menace or someone who would play stickball.

"My brother actually is dying," I said. "I wasn't joking the other day."

"I kind of figured," he said. "I'm sorry."

"It's okay. It's just one of those things."

"It's still got to suck."

"It does suck," I said. "I thought we were helping him get better, but now I'm not so sure."

"Here, I'll walk you to the bus. Maybe you can meet Noodle sometime."

On Monday, after school, Francie and I were back at the mall together as if nothing had happened. I guess Francie didn't know anything had happened at all. We rode the bus and made our way up the grassy hill together like always. We stood in front of the glowing map of the mall, running our fingers across the geometric, chalky-colored legends, debating our first hit of the afternoon.

"It's been a while since Bebe has seen these faces," Francie said. "Shall we remind them who's boss?"

"I don't care if I never see another Bebe dress as long as I live," I said. "All those feathers and sequins. Ugh."

"Well, where do you want to go?" she asked.

I closed my eyes and pointed. When I opened them, Francie was checking my selection against the directory. "B-thirteen. Great, Val. Mrs. Bigger's. Awesome choice."

"It's a change of pace, at least. And you never know—maybe we'll be fat someday and a fat-dress will come in handy."

I didn't tell her I had seen Max without her. It's not like I had done anything wrong. I mean, I hadn't, had I? Just a few weeks before, she had made it clear that she wasn't trying to get down with him herself. And neither was I, for that matter. All I had done was have a conversation. But I still felt—in some small, nagging way—like I had betrayed Francie. Maybe just because she was supposed to be all that I needed. We were supposed to have a world of our own, with no use for anyone outside the two of us. By hanging alone with Max, I was letting someone else in, and without Francie's permission or knowledge. I was lapsing in my service to Francie's ultimate goal:

We're going to do it, Val. The two of us. You start small and expand the operation. A piece at a time, a piece at a time. Start with a charm bracelet. Move on to the Great Pyramids. It will take both of us. I am asking for your undivided loyalty. But someday it's all going to be ours. Every single thing.

She had asked me for my allegiance. That was all that Francie had ever required of me. She had put her ass on the line for me. I wondered if I had let her down.

I wondered if I had done it on purpose.

Chapter Eighteen

One day, after Physics class, I stayed behind. Ms. Tinker didn't notice me at first; she was too busy puttering around at her desk, gathering up papers and rearranging things for the next class. But I hovered at the edge of her desk until she finally looked up and saw me. "Vincenza," she greeted me. "What can I do ya for?"

I ignored her mistake. There was no point, and anyway, I was pretty sure by then that it wasn't a mistake at all. "I wanted to ask you something," I said.

"No such thing as a smart question," she clucked. I was aware of her stance on questions. It was Classroom Policy #4. There Is No Such Thing as a Smart Question—Only Smart Answers.

"I just wanted to know—when I saw you in the mall

that day. In Ann Taylor Loft. How did you know about the Sign?"

"Can't have been me. I've never been to the mall," Ms. Tinker said, averting her gaze. "I do all my shopping at craft fairs. Where do you think I got this?" She tipped her purple beret at me. "You can't find something like this at the mall, now can you?"

"Just the same," I said. "I know I saw you there. And you gave me the Sign. I'm sure of it."

"Hmm," she mused. "Very interesting. Do you like physics?"

"Not really," I admitted.

"I knew you would. Physics is phun, and you're one of my best students. I think this will interest you." Her left eye twitched. She took a piece of chalk and pranced over to the blackboard, where she began to write out a long, complicated equation that I didn't understand at all.

She pulled her fist back and forth across the blackboard and, as if by magic, neat white rows began to appear. Numbers and symbols, but also hearts and stars and clouds, none of it in any intelligible configuration. I found myself squinting, trying to make sense of it all. I was far from Ms. Tinker's best student, but even I knew enough to know that a heart is not an accepted symbol used in physics.

Ms. Tinker was humming a cheerful, bouncing little tune. Finally, when there was no more space on the blackboard, she finished it all off with a giant equal sign and a smiley face, which she circled several times before she turned around and faced me victoriously.

"I don't get it," I said.

"That's because it's meaningless!" she exclaimed, pleased with herself. "Physics teaches us many things. But I don't really understand physics. I used to be a special education teacher, you know. There's not a lot of physics in special ed."

"If you say so," I said.

"I'm just an old woman," Ms. Tinker went on. "I believe that there is no such thing as a smart question. But one thing I have learned about physics—this was in the teacher's manual—is that the answers are always right in front of your face. Asking questions just shows that you don't care enough about the answers to figure them out for yourself. Does that make sense?"

"Sort of," I said. "I mean, no, but maybe."

"You can't learn a lot in school," Ms. Tinker said. "That's why I mostly focus on making sure everyone's notebook holes are reinforced. What else am I supposed to grade on?"

"Um," I said. If she was trying to make herself seem more reasonable, she was failing.

"No one can answer anything for you," Ms. Tinker said. "Especially me. I'm just going by the teacher's manual, anyway. What do I know? Well, I know a few things, but none of them have to do with physics. I know about felting. I know how to speak a little bit of Flemish. That's not very useful; hardly anyone speaks Flemish, except maybe your friend Francie."

"Why would Francie speak Flemish?" I asked.

Ms. Tinker giggled mischievously. "Let's just say I have good reason to believe that your dear friend might be a robot. Or a hologram. Have you seen the outfits she wears?"

"This conversation makes no sense," I said. "Are you for real?"

She cackled and pushed her glasses up on the end of her pointy nose. "If I wasn't, would it make a difference? It's all the same in the end. The teacher's manual says that up to three-quarters of physics is belief. It's what you believe that matters. If Newton hadn't believed in gravity, where would we be now?"

"Where?"

"Floating around in outer space, that's where!" she yelped in exasperation.

"I guess," I said.

"Don't be foolish. You know I can't abide foolishness," Ms. Tinker reminded me.

She tugged on one earlobe, then another, and twitched her nose, and bared her teeth in a toothy brown grin. I didn't make the Sign back. I left the classroom, unsure of whether Ms. Tinker had told me anything at all. I guess there's no such thing as a smart question.

The next day we had a substitute, and again the next. A

week later, with no explanation, we heard that Ms. Tinker would not be returning to Sandra Dee.

Francie and I met at the subway later that day. We had been collecting stuff for Jesse for a while now, and it was starting to build up. I'd brought a few things for him when I'd visited, and sent some of it with Liz when she went to visit him, but I couldn't deliver it nearly as fast as we were stealing it. We had to make a big drop.

Francie arrived at the station in gold stiletto sandals that laced all the way up her calves, denim cutoffs so short that they revealed the lowermost curve of her ass, and a skintight Smiths concert T-shirt that she had cropped right above her belly button. She had her hair pulled away from her face with a pronged, metallic headband.

"You look like a total slut," I told her. "A slutty pineapple."

"I look beautiful," she said. "What's wrong with looking like a slut, anyway? I don't see why people always criticize. I thought everyone liked sluts! Did you bring the stuff?"

But what I was really thinking was that she looked different these days. Still slutty, just different. While she'd always cultivated that unkempt, greasy style, today she just looked kind of dirty, like she hadn't showered in a week. Her eyeliner was crooked and crusted over. And there was something desperate in her eyes, in her tone of voice. It was like she was trying too hard; like she knew she had to struggle at what had always come so easily to her.

I opened the duffel bag I was carrying and showed Francie the loot. It was everything we had stolen for Jesse over the past couple of weeks. This time I'd warned him we were coming.

"You know, you don't have to come with me to Jesse's just to be nice," I told Francie. "I could do it myself if you want."

"Babe," Francie said. "You think I'm coming to be *nice*? What planet are you on?"

"I know. But you don't have to. I just want you to know."

"I definitely want to. I know I can convert him," Francie said.

"I thought you didn't have time for boys."

"Exactly. *Boys*. Jesse is clearly one hundred million percent *man*."

I hated how Francie was always talking about how hot Jesse was, and not just because he was my brother, either. There was something that seemed thoughtless about it, as if she was willfully forgetting the truth of the situation, or even making fun of it. Francie was the one who was always looking for the Most Beautiful Thing. Francie knew from beautiful. And it seemed to me that she of all people should be able to see that even if Jesse still looked okay on the outside, he could never really be beautiful again. But maybe Francie was seeing something else entirely.

"Well, good luck with that," I said. "You'll look good in widow's weeds."

Francie gave me a cross, regretful frown. "Don't talk that way," she said. "Look at everything we have for him. It may not be the Holy Grail, but for now it's enough."

"I'm starting to wonder," I said.

"You can't wonder," Francie said.

Jesse was on the couch when we got to his place. He had actually cleaned it up, if only slightly. "Hey, Hot Stuff," Francie gushed.

"Hey, Sexy," Jesse responded.

She left her glossy mark on his forehead.

"I love your apartment," she told him. She was taking it upon herself to inspect it, standing at the window examining the architecture, knocking on the plaster walls, looking for signs of sturdiness. "Someday I'm going to have a place just like this."

"I love your outfit," Jesse said. His voice was froggy.

"Valentina thinks I look like a slut."

"Nothing wrong with that," Jesse said.

"That's what I said."

No one had said a word to me. It was as if I wasn't even in the room. I examined the chips in my nail polish while Francie cuddled up to an amused Jesse and threw her arm around his neck.

I spoke up. "We brought you some stuff."

"More booze, huh?"

"Not exactly." I opened up the duffel bag and dumped the contents out onto the floor. The hats, the tank tops, the books, the toys; all of it was there. We had been collecting it.

"Awesome. Thanks. So remind me why you guys are always giving me this stuff?"

"Don't ask so many questions," Francie snapped with good nature. "Look!" She pulled the Brookstone flashlight from the pile. "A hand-crank flashlight. So you will never be without light. It charges your cell phone, too; you just need to get the attachment separate. What kind of cell phone do you have?"

"It's a Nokia," he said.

"I'll see if I can get you the right thingy," she said. "I bet they have them at Radio Shack. I don't know about you, but my phone is always running out of batteries."

"You're awful," Jesse said. "Stealing all this stuff. Luring my innocent little sister into your shadowy underworld."

Francie flipped her hair and used her arms to push her boobs up and forward, practically to her shoulders. "It's not my fault I have a gift," she said.

"You have many gifts," he replied. "Look at all this stuff. How much would it have cost?"

"Close to six hundred dollars," Francie said. "I did a spreadsheet in Excel."

Jesse still hadn't gotten up off the couch. Francie mussed his hair and was examining his face without shame. He had not changed. Even with the gifts, he still looked like shit. Something had gone wrong. And I saw a quiver in Francie's lower lip, a failure of confidence, as she realized it for herself.

"Don't you like it?" she asked.

"I love it," he said. It didn't really sound like he was there.

I wanted to be surprised, but for some reason I wasn't. I'd heard somewhere that up to three quarters of physics is belief.

Francie stood without taking her eyes off him, and you could tell the wheels were turning in her head, trying to figure out what was happening. I'm not sure she'd ever believed me before when I'd told her he was dying. But now it was obvious. His eyes were fluttering open and shut like he was about to fall asleep. You could see his rib cage vibrating through his T-shirt.

Francie looked up at me, flailing.

If up to three-quarters of physics is belief, then what's the other quarter? I guess it's just physics.

"Maybe we should go," I said.

"Sorry," Jesse said. "I just got really sleepy all of a sudden."

"It's cool," I said.

Francie didn't talk much on the street outside. She took slow, narrow steps down the sidewalk, her heels clomping awkwardly. "Things are changing," she said after a while. We were cutting through the circle on the way to the subway, looping around the fountain. "I can feel things changing. Not just the weather, either, even if that's part of it. I get this feeling now and then."

I snorted. "Ha!" I said. "Now you're psychic? Like what exactly is changing?"

"I can't explain it," Francie said. "But I guess it's something like a new chapter starting. Don't you have, like, this sense of the unknown lately? Usually I have, like, a general feeling about where things are heading, but for the past few weeks I just have no idea at all."

"I hope it's heading somewhere good."

"It usually isn't," she sighed.

We walked along together. Francie's hair was blowing wild. We made our way through the park and across the street, where a new building was going up. "I wonder what used to be there?" Francie asked.

I wasn't going to give her an answer, because I had none, but I wouldn't have had time anyway, because a bunch of construction workers suddenly started yelling at her from the building site.

"Look out, Blondie," a dude called. "You got all your snacks hanging out the back!"

"You're beautiful!"

"Wanna have my baby?"

You'd think she would have been used to it. That kind of thing would only have amused her before. But that day Francie froze at the catcalls. She stopped and turned, facing the guys who were shouting at her, but said nothing. Her shoulders dropped. She just stood there.

"Francie, come on," I said. "Don't listen to them. They're just assholes."

She looked over her shoulder at me, still frozen in one spot. The guys, emboldened, were coming closer.

"Lemme smell your panties!"

"You like it rough, don't you, baby?"

"You've got a pretty face. Wanna sit on mine?"

I touched Francie's shoulder. She was breathing hard. "Francie," I said. "Come on. Let's get out of here."

"I can't," Francie said. There was panic in her voice.

"What?"

"I can't move," Francie said. "There's something wrong with my legs."

The guys were circling now, only a few feet away. They looked kind of nervous, too, like they'd never taken it this far before but knew that they couldn't turn back. "What about your friend?" one of them asked. "Is she a slut like you?"

I had to do something. Francie wouldn't move. So I stepped out in front of her, my feet wide, my shoulders square. I felt a certain blackness behind my eyes. I was not afraid. "Fuck you all," I said quietly. There was really no need to shout. "Really, fuck you all. She's fourteen fucking years old."

"Fifteen next month," Francie managed to wheeze, but I don't think they heard her.

That was all it took. I'd barely said anything, hadn't even raised my voice, but I looked each of them right in the eye, and as I looked each of them in the eye, an absence crossed their faces, like they had forgotten why they were even there at all. "Sorry," the fattest one said. "Only playing around." And just like that, they all wandered off listlessly, back to work, leaving us.

Francie sat down in the middle of the sidewalk and covered her mouth and nose with her hands. The street was completely empty; it was just us. "Francie," I said. "Are you okay?" She didn't answer. She sat there like that for a few minutes, then gathered herself up, and we headed on our way.

When we finally sat down on the subway, Francie couldn't look me in the eye. "Thank you," she said. "I don't know what happened. You saved my ass."

And I knew I should have tried to comfort her. But I didn't want to. She had disappointed me. "I told you you looked like a hooker," I said. "Maybe you should have listened to me."

"I'm sorry," Francie said. She was crying now. "I should have listened."

Chapter Nineteen

At ten o'clock, Max was outside my bedroom window throwing rocks.

"You know, they invented cell phones for a reason," I whispered when I met him at the back door. "You should have just called. This is some *Leave It to Beaver* bullshit."

"I don't have your cell number," said Max. "Or I would have called. I'm just glad that was your window and not your parents'. I had to guess."

I led him upstairs to my room and turned on some music to cover our voices, then pulled the computer chair away from my desk for him and sat on the edge of my bed.

"What are you doing here?" I asked.

"I don't know," he said. "I smoked a J and decided to go for a bike ride. And now I'm here."

"Don't you have parents?" I asked.

"No one has parents around here."

"True," I said.

We sat there looking at each other for what felt like a really long time.

"So what's up?" I asked.

"Not much," Max said. "You look different or something. Every time I see you you look different from before."

"Thanks." I took it as a compliment.

"You *seem* different," he said.

"Well, maybe I am."

And he rolled his chair across the wood floor and kissed me. He just did. I kissed him back. What else could I do?

Kissing Max was pleasant, but not, like, out of control or anything. I had never kissed anyone before—besides Francie, who didn't count—and I have to admit I was expecting it to be more exciting. When I had kissed Francie, it had been a solemn agreement between the two of us. Like pricking our thumbs and rubbing the blood together. But with Max, it was all spit and wiggling tongues. I thought of a quiz I'd once taken in *Seventeen* magazine. "Are You a Good Kisser?" With Max's open mouth against mine, his hand inching up my thigh, I wanted to know: What is the difference? What would a good kisser be doing that I wasn't? I tried to think back to the quiz, but all I could remember was something about sweaty palms. My palms weren't sweaty. Was that good or bad? I couldn't remember.

"So what's your phone number, anyway?" Max asked when I broke away. "It's kind of weird that I don't actually have it." I gave him the number, he tapped it into his phone, and then he disappeared.

Weird, I thought. And I stood up and looked at myself in the mirror and smoothed my hair. *So that's what it's like.*

After school the next day, Francie was in the bleachers, alone, clutching her cigarette like it was heavier than her entire body. It was spring, and 70, and from where I stood on the sidewalk, the blossoms that had fallen from the trees were whirling everywhere in little eddies of wind. I watched her for a few minutes from across the football field before walking in the other direction. She didn't see me.

Chapter Twenty

*L*iz came to take me out on a chilly Sunday afternoon, gray and overcast, at the end of April. I wasn't expecting her. The thing about Liz is that while I definitely admired her, and appreciated all the clothes she let us steal, I didn't exactly like her. She had a way of making me feel uncomfortable. Given a choice, I probably would not have chosen to spend an afternoon with her.

You don't always get a choice. When Liz came to pick me up, she was dressed like an old-fashioned movie star, with a silk polka-dotted scarf tied over her head and red cat's-eye sunglasses. But her lips were chapped, and puffy bags peered out from the lower rims of her glasses.

I tried to think of an excuse not to go with her, but I couldn't come up with one. So I got into her little blue

Volkswagen, which had probably been paid for with hocked Gap merchandise, and we drove off.

She took me ice-skating at the mall. "Just you and me," she'd said. It turned out that Liz had been halfway decent at skating once, when she was my age, but she'd given it up because her parents weren't about to pay for coaches and tutus and everything. It was just as well, Liz said. Who wants to be fat, insane, and broke, all for the sake of one double axel at age sixteen?

"I'm moving to Australia soon," she informed me when we were on the rink, just skating around and around, me grabbing her hip every now and then for balance. She had taken off the scarf and sunglasses as soon as we'd gotten out of the car. I guess she had realized for herself how absurd she looked.

"What are you going to do in Australia, of all places?" I asked her.

"I'm gonna break into the soaps. They're big there, you know. *Neighbors* and all. They call it *Naybas*. Maybe I'll meet a man with an Australian accent. It's all I ask."

"That's dumb," I told her.

"I know," she said. "Ridiculous, right? But something ridiculous is the only thing left to do. And I love kangaroos. So cute."

"When are you going?" I wanted to know.

"After . . . you know."

"After Jesse dies."

"Right." She gave me an apologetic shrug, did a little

pivot on her skates, and suddenly she was skating backward, facing me. "I mean, he's the reason I even came back from LA in the first place, obviously. It hasn't done much good. I don't see him any more than you do. I think he's avoiding me for some reason. But at least he knows I'm here. If he needs me, I'm here."

"Why are you telling me this?" I asked her.

"I guess I just wanted to say good-bye. Because when it happens, there's not going to be time. We're all going to be preoccupied with other stuff."

"I guess."

"It's going to be soon," Liz said. She looked at me hard. "I want you to be prepared. You remind me of myself, I think." She took my hand and twirled me under the strong arch of her bicep. "I thought I could save him, but I couldn't. You can't, either. You know that, right?"

We'd done twenty or thirty laps of the rink at this point. We had passed this spot so many times that it seemed like we hadn't ever left it.

"I'd stay, but I can't," Liz said. "And anyway, what good am I? I couldn't help Jesse. I spent years trying to help him, if you want the truth. Even before he got sick. Look where it got him."

"What is he even sick with?" I finally asked. It was the question that everyone always avoided.

"I think he's just bored," Liz said. "I mean, that's as good a guess as any, right?"

"Last I checked, you couldn't die of boredom."

"What, I look like a doctor?"

I shrugged. "It just seems like a dumb reason to die."

"Well, obviously it's more complicated, but you know what I'm saying. And really, the important part—the true, actual thing of all of it—is that it does not fucking matter. Jesse has made his own choices, cowardly and pathetic though they may have been. It's all on him, okay? None of us could have done anything. I told you, I tried. I even went to a witch doctor in New Orleans and bought a crystal and tied a piece of his hair around it and threw it in the ocean."

"Sucker," I snorted.

"Tell me about it. That crystal was really fucking expensive."

Then she left me, wobbling on the ice, to skate out to the eye of the rink, where there was a circle drawn for fanciness. There, Liz twirled and leaped while some schlocky old song played, narrowly dodging little kids and red-jacketed guards, while I retreated to the bleachers and bummed a Marlboro Light from an old lady.

I watched Liz skate. She had gone off like a bomb—detonated by a sequence of familiar twitches. She'd thought she wouldn't remember how to do it; she hadn't skated in years. But her body still knew, I guess, because she flew through the air with an instinct so killer that I was almost afraid to watch.

Liz stabbed the ice with the picks on her toes, threw her arms like helicopter blades before liftoff. Flakes of ice sparking from her feet. It reminded me somehow of Francie. No— of myself. I wondered if I'd always remember how to steal. I pictured myself years in the future, reclaiming that sneaky art with a screaming baby in one hand and a bag of cat food in the other, in the crowded aisle of a supermarket. It would always be with me, I realized. When I was ready, I could let it go.

But I wasn't ready. Not quite yet.

I watched Liz spin and spin in the center of the rink, that girl a cold blur of fury and resentment and determination. She was spinning faster and faster, and then, just like that, she transformed. She was all ice. She was like me. And I realized suddenly that I'd been mistaken all along. I had been relying on Francie. But Francie would never be enough. It wasn't her fault—no one else could ever be enough. If Liz had taught me anything that day, it was that I had only myself to rely on.

Anyway, Francie was less extraordinary every day. Something had caused her illusion to fray at the edges, and it seemed that it might begin to unravel completely at any time. As for me: there in the bleachers, burning through that Marlboro Light, I knew that I was only growing stronger. I was more beautiful with every breath. Francie was not going to rescue me, or my brother, or anyone. I had to do it myself. It was so obvious. I don't know how I'd ever seen it any other way. I was not ready to give up yet. I was more beautiful than ever.

The next day, Monday, I passed Francie a note in the class that was no longer Ms. Tinker's, telling her I couldn't go to the mall. *Too much shit to do,* the note said. She just turned around and shrugged.

I went to Jesse's by myself, just because, bearing a pair of cheap drugstore sunglasses as a tiny offering. By then it was tradition. The route to my brother's place was becoming as familiar as the one to the mall, and when I got there I didn't even say hello, just climbed onto the couch next to him and curled up, perched the sunglasses on his brow.

"I'm not sure if we're both going to fit like this," he croaked. He was right. My ass was hanging off the edge.

"I'll scrunch."

"Robin Hood," he murmured, "you are, like, so full of fearlessness that I can hardly stand it."

"And all this time I thought you knew what you were talking about," I said.

On Jesse's couch I felt like a fetus, all pink translucence and no fingernails. He was so much older than me. Old enough to be dying.

We just lay there, my arms wrapped around his chest, his body suddenly as fragile as the little piece of vibrating tissue paper in a kazoo.

Francie could not save him. All she had done was cast

one of her many illusions. But I didn't need Francie anymore. I was going to accomplish what she had failed.

Have you ever done that thing where you take a hand mirror and hold it up to, say, the mirror on the medicine cabinet, and turn it an inch in this direction, an inch in that direction, until you've got the angle just right so that you see an endless string of yourself reflected back in front of you, into infinity? That was how I felt looking at Jesse that night. He was my brother. If I had been nine years older, we could have been twins. We could have been the same person. We were mirrors, pushed together face-to-face on his threadbare couch, eyes open, my hand on his shoulder. And looking at my older brother that night, saying nothing, there was a spark of understanding, and instantly I could see both myself and him, reflected back in a mysterious, repeating line that stretched through all the years. All the versions of ourselves that we had ever known, an infinite loop.

That night, I fell asleep with my brother on the couch, my face planted in his armpit, the ceiling fan whizzing steadily in time with our breathing. And I drifted off that night with the surest feeling—the most unwavering, irrational certitude—that everything was going to be okay.

Chapter Twenty-one

Sometime later, it was midnight, and Max was over again.

He had started showing up more and more lately. Sometimes he showed up at night. Other times I'd tell Francie I had to study and he'd come over straightaway after school. He had been here last night, too, and three nights before, and the afternoon before that, too, never with any clear purpose beyond the obvious. He wasn't usually that intent on the obvious, either.

In some ways it was actually pretty annoying. I had things to do: homework, a shower, um, sleep. Yeah, I was, like, somewhat in love with him, or whatever, but that only goes so far. It would have been different if we'd had anything to talk about. But Max's secret late-night visits were usually about

75 percent silence, 24 percent chitchat, and 1 percent makeout session. Sometimes we snuck out to the backyard and smoked a bowl, and didn't talk out there, either.

Sometimes I wanted to say, *Max, it's a school night.* I wanted to ask, *Max, what do you want from me, anyway?* Or *Why don't we cut this bullshit here and get right to the good part?*

But there were things I liked about him, too. He was sort of funny. He was smart, and weirdly tough. Despite his pathological distractability, I knew that he had the best intentions. Plus he was hot. It was all of that.

Of course, that stuff's not all that important. Anyone can be smart and funny and a slightly good person. Actually I would say that most people probably are. Others are hot on top of it all, too. It's rare, I guess, but not, like, anything to get all excited about.

No. What I liked most about Max was this: he was him and I was me. He wasn't trying to change anything. He didn't want me to be anything more to him than a sort of girlfriend. He expected very little from me. I could walk away at any moment—he could walk away—and neither of us would take a piece of the other with us. He was just Max. I was Valentina Martinez.

That night he was lying on my floor, amid laundry and CDs and year-old fashion magazines. He had his arms flung over his head, T-shirt riding up to reveal the tan, flat stomach, the thin line of darkness leading into his jeans. He seemed to be staring at the glow-in-the-dark stars on my ceiling, even though the lights were on and you could barely see him. I was staring at him. We were both staring. He was beautiful.

And this time when he kissed me, I was ready for it. We had kissed a lot since his first visit a few weeks ago. It never lasted for more than three minutes, give or take two and a half minutes. He sat on my bed, with his hands on my hips and mine on his shoulders, and inched his way up to my boob as we chewed on each other's lips. Even though I know you're not supposed to open your eyes when you're kissing someone, I let my lids drift open, and I saw him staring back at me.

We stared at each other like that for a few seconds, pupils only millimeters away, and his tongue down my throat the whole time. Caught in the intensity of his glance, I felt nervous. I had to laugh and pull back.

He grabbed my wrist and pulled me back on top of him. "Let's have sex," he said. "I brought a condom."

It felt like my eyes might pop out of my head.

"Uh, no!" I said.

"Why not?"

"We can't even figure out how to kiss right. And now you want to start doing it?"

"We were kissing fine."

Max pulled his shirt off. His body was tan and muscled and perfect, his collarbone jutting out from between his shoulders in a smooth and undeviating ridge. I wish I could say that I kicked him out right there, that this was the final straw. But I couldn't help faltering. Max on my bed looking at once predatory and unbearably vulnerable. His lips half parted, blue eyes wide and implying a million things all at the same time. He ran a hand through his hair self-consciously, but didn't try to move any closer.

He looked sexy, okay?

"Come on," he said.

I didn't want to hurt his feelings. Max seemed like the kind of person whose feelings were easily bruised. But I couldn't do it. It wasn't that I was being precious about my so-called virginity, because really, the thing to do about *that* seemed to be to get it over with. It was something else.

"You don't really want to," I said.

"Yes I do. Why would I be sitting here like this if I didn't want to do it?"

"I don't mean it that way," I said. "It's just that if I have sex with someone, I kind of want it to have something to do with me. I'm not sure that this has anything to do with me at all."

"That's the most retarded thing I ever heard," he said. "How could it not have to do with you? If it didn't have to do with you, I'd just be jerking off, right?"

It was no surprise that he didn't get it. "Just put your shirt on."

He didn't move at first, but then he stood, and then,

arms across his chest, he was dressed. He turned his back to me.

"Don't be mad," I said.

He tilted his chin in my direction, but he was still only half facing me. "You want to know what I think?" he asked. All I could make of his expression was a flicker of eyelash.

"What?"

"I think this has to do with Francie," he said.

"It's just . . ." I started. But I didn't know how to finish the thought. He had caught me off guard.

"Am I wrong?" he said.

"I'm not a lesbo," I replied.

Max rolled his eyes. "You don't understand what I'm saying at all."

From my window I watched Max's bike drift through the night, a lazy arrow of unformed intention shooting toward a target that neither of us could know. I wondered if I would ever see him again, and then realized that with Max, the uncertainty was in itself something of a guarantee.

Chapter Twenty-two

Things were getting out of control. I hadn't seen Max in a week or so and Francie and I were back to going to the mall every day. I could not stop stealing.

Before, at the mall, I'd held Francie in my mind at every step. I could be at Claire's, facing the wall of earrings, and know, with absolute certainty, exactly what Francie was doing in the opposite corner of the store. I could always feel her electricity, know the precise path of her hands as they grabbed and grabbed. Her heat was always burning on the back of my neck.

Now that heat was gone, and I just, truly, didn't care. Francie could tag along with me if she wanted, but we were each doing our own thing, and what Francie's *thing* was, if she even had one, was no longer my concern.

In Bloomingdale's with Francie in the spring, the tables were overflowing with things that I could take. Comfortable wool sweaters; long, scented candles and bottles of translucent blue bubble bath; a set of good cutlery; and a Belgian waffle iron with six settings. What was the point, because it wasn't going to help anything anyway. But there must have been a point, because I went a little overboard.

"I think Julia Child is my shopping partner," Francie said, as we rode the escalator down to Intimates. "What do you want with fancy cooking knives?"

"I just like them. They're sharp, okay?"

"Maybe you shouldn't take anything else. You've got a good haul," Francie said.

"Maybe you should leave me alone," I told her. "Maybe you got me into this in the first place."

"Well, fuck you, too," Francie said without conviction.

We didn't say anything after that, but we both knew how it was. Walking through the racks of bras, we were quiet.

In the beginning it had been Francie's idea to start stealing. We were going to steal everything. But the thing is, we had not made a dent; we had amassed thousands of dollars worth of complete junk only to find ourselves right where we started. No one had noticed our efforts. The racks and shelves of the mall were still overflowing.

Somehow it just made me want to take more. Somehow the futility of it was exactly what made it so important. When you take on an impossible goal, you first have to accept certain impossibilities as premise, and when those impossibilities prove impossible, you throw your own talents back at them.

That day at the mall, Francie didn't look great. She'd stolen these genuine-fur eyelashes from Eyelash Bar, and had caked mascara and eyeliner on top of them until they were clumpy and crusty. She was wearing plastic rings on every finger, but they were dull and cheap-looking, like she'd gotten them with quarters from dispensers at the supermarket, which I happened to know she had.

Francie knew something was wrong. You could tell from the way she moved, all tentative and jittery. You could tell from the way she deferred to me at every turn, always asking what I thought about one thing or the other, and waiting for my answers with fidgety uncertainty. She stole with a dim, flickering glow and a nervous look in her eyes. I worried she would be caught any day, and wondered what I would do if it happened.

We walked through the mall together, side by side, but really by ourselves. I could sense Francie looking at me, again and again, out of the corner of her eye. When we passed one of those freestanding kiosks that sells those personalized nameplate necklaces, she just reached out and plucked one from the rack. We kept on walking.

"Jennifer," Francie said, holding the nameplate up to her chest. "What do you think of me as a Jennifer?"

"I don't know if it works," I said. "I can't think of a

name that would fit you as well as Francie. Maybe *DeeDee*. I don't know."

"I wonder if I would be different as a Jennifer," Francie said, fastening the nameplate around her neck. "Like, if I had been born Jennifer and raised that way, would my life be any different?"

"Of course not," I said. "That's ridiculous. What's that thing they say about a rose is a rose is a rose?"

"Well . . ." Francie said. She seemed to really be considering it. The corner of her mouth was twitching ever so slightly. There was a small, barely noticeable catch in her voice. "I read Gertrude Stein over the summer and it's hard to know exactly what she meant when she wrote that. I mean, you can take it a couple of different ways. She was crazy anyway, so who cares what she thinks? I am not a rose, and if my name was Jennifer, I think I would probably be a happier person. Or better yet! *Jenny*. If I was Jenny, don't you suppose I would be sort of pleasantly plump and always smiling?"

"If you say so, Francie," I said.

"Jenny," she corrected me. She had reclaimed her composure. "It's Jenny from now on."

We went to visit Liz at the Gap.

"Where you been all my life?" Liz called from a ladder by the denim wall. Francie and I sauntered over, and Liz climbed down from her perch, carrying a pair of jeans that someone had left crumpled in a little ball. Liz laid the jeans on top of a pile of T-shirts and began to fold.

"It's been ages," Liz said. "I thought maybe you guys had reformed your ways or something."

"Nah," I said. "We've been around."

"Well, I've been holding a bunch of stuff for you. I think you'll like it." Liz winked at Francie.

"Goody," Francie said. "I'll be back in a second." She marched off to the bathroom to retrieve the loot that Liz had stashed for us there.

"She looks like shit," Liz said when Francie was out of earshot. "Did something happen?"

"Not that I know of." I shrugged. I was watching Liz fold the jeans. She would fold them perfectly, then let them fall to the floor, then pick them up and fold them all over again. Fold, drop, fold, drop, fold. Repeat.

"I would watch out for her," Liz said. "A girl like Francie starts letting herself go and something's not right."

But when Francie came back only a few minutes later, she was back to her old self, buoyed by the stolen Gap merchandise. She waltzed up to me and Liz, her shopping bag swinging with a new weightiness, her JENNIFER nameplate gold and sparkly. Francie's hair was now impeccably tousled, the lines of her makeup were smooth and finely drawn, and her boobs were perky and bouncy in a tight black bustier. She looked taller than ever on six-inch patent-leather heels. Liz didn't seem to notice the difference.

"Come on," Francie said. "Let's get out of here." She wiggled her bag in the direction of the exit, and we floated away, past the clerks at the cash register, past the mulish customers with all their stupid questions, and through the beeping sensors at the front of the store, out into the mall.

As we left, I could hear Liz saying, "Oh, you must be mistaken. I know those girls."

On the escalator I looked up at Francie, standing tall. Francie, who could do anything, who had been sent to me to change something. Strange visitor. I trusted her. For a few minutes, it was just like it used to be.

Francie and I breezed along, up the escalators to the top floor, heady with the thrill of theft. The shopping-mall air was cool and fragrant with that smell I recognized from before I had met her: cinnamon, makeup, the future. Francie in the bustier, the miniskirt. Long, long legs. Me in my motorcycle jacket. We may not have looked alike, but Francie and I were sisters, like it or not.

We stood next to each other on the balcony, looking out over everything that was already ours. From up there, the shoppers on the ground floor looked like . . . I don't know. They didn't look like ants. They looked like what they were, which is tiny people. And me and Francie—towering over them—we were giants. If I had wanted to, I knew, I could have reached down and picked any one of them up and flung them clear from one end of the mall to the other. Flicked them like marbles. But that was not what I wanted to do. I was a benevolent god.

Francie pulled a hair band out from somewhere inside her bustier and wrapped her hair into a lazy topknot.

"Why are you so mad at me?" she asked.

"I'm not mad at you," I said.

She rested her hand on my chest, the flat part right under my clavicle. "Be straight with me, Val. I'm a clever bitch. I can tell something's wrong."

"We can be friends without having to, like, share a brain," I said. "It doesn't mean I'm mad at you or anything like that."

She was speechless at that. "I don't know what I would do without you," she finally said.

"What do you mean?"

"I don't think you realize how lonely I was," she said. "I mean, sometimes I would go for days without speaking to a single person except Sandy. Can you even imagine?"

"Francie, come on," I said. She dropped her hands to her side and turned away.

"And I don't know what I did," she said. "I must have done something, though, right? All this—" She fluttered her hand in that way she had. "Did I do something to piss you off? I mean, I don't know what I did, and if I did something, it was legitimately not on purpose, so just tell me and I'll make it up to you." She searched me, imploring, and tugged at the *JENNIFER* nameplate around her neck.

"Francie," I said. "It's nothing."

"I thought you could protect me," Francie said. "From

the minute I saw you in Ms. Tinker's class, I said to myself, There is a girl who has been through some shit and come out harder on the other side. There is a girl who is untouchable. Someone with certain weapons at her disposal. Someone who can love something and keep it safe."

"You always said *you* were going to protect *me*," I said, shocked at her admission.

"Yeah," she said. "I did say that. And haven't I held up my end of the bargain?"

We took the J-12 home. On the bus I listened to the hum of the engine and wondered why I was so angry at Francie, and why her honesty had made me all the angrier. I tried to close my eyes and picture the scenery crawling by, tried to ground myself in the familiar rhythm of the traffic lights, but I couldn't concentrate.

"My brother is dying," I finally said. "Everyone seems to think it's just this done deal, that there's nothing we can do."

"There are things you can change and things you can't," Francie said.

"Maybe there are things that *you* can't change," I said. "But I'm going to find it. Maybe you've given up. I thought you were better than that, but I guess I was wrong. And I am going to find it."

"Find what?"

"The Most Beautiful Thing," I said. "The Holy Grail."

Francie looked at me like she was sad to discover exactly

how fucking insane I really was. She laid her head down across my lap, right there on the bus, looking up, her face wide and open and exhausted. She stretched one arm out into the aisle and put the other one around my shoulder, arched her back. "Val," she said. "I am telling you this for your own good. We're not going to find the Holy Grail. We're not going to steal the Grand Canyon, or the Declaration of Independence, or even *one* of Marie Antoinette's wigs, or anything like that. There are a lot of things we're not going to do. I mean, I was just playing around."

She gave me a sheepish wince, like it was the most obvious, unavoidable truth, like she just couldn't hide it anymore but knew I would understand.

That was the biggest betrayal of all: the fact that she didn't even realize it was a betrayal.

"Fuck you, Francie," I said. The bus was just pulling to a stop, and I pushed her off of me and stood up, gathering my things as quickly as I could. I climbed from the bus into an unknown neighborhood, miles from home. From the middle of the deserted street I called Max.

"Dude," he said when he answered. "You're crying. What the hell?"

"I don't know," I said. "I don't know. Things are, like, getting kind of out of control, I think."

I sat in the bus shelter but didn't get on any of the buses that passed by. I just waited.

And I wondered about things. I was starting to realize

that I had questions; things that I had never considered before.

Questions like:

What if my brother was going to die? What if Liz was going to Australia? What if Max had no use for me anymore? And what if, what if, what if? What if Francie had never been at all what she seemed? What if I was alone?

Maybe I was alone. But my brother would not die. Everyone else had given up, if they were even trying in the first place. I would not give up.

After an hour or so I saw Max appear as a distant speck, gliding toward me on his skateboard.

"Hey," he said, making a messy stop in front of me, flipping his board up onto its end.

"Hey," I said.

He sat down next to me, and we both stared out at the traffic. "I'm glad you called," he said. "I didn't know if you were going to. I mean, like, ever. Is everything all right?"

"I'm sorry about the other night."

"Me too. I shouldn't have acted like that. Like you're some slut. You have your principles. It's cool."

"It's not principles," I sighed. "I don't believe in principles. It's just . . . let's just forget it."

"Forgotten," Max said. He reached out and touched my hand, then grabbed it and placed it under his, on my knee. "What's the matter, anyway?"

"Francie's just a fucking liar," I said.

"You let her boss you around too much," he said.

"That's not it at all," I told him.

"Well, I still think you give her too much credit," he said. "You're not as helpless as you think you are. I kinda don't think you ever have been. Here, have a drink." He pulled a small metal flask from his pocket and took a swig, then offered it to me. Floppy blond hair flirting with long dark eyelashes. When I touched the flask to my lips, I could still taste him on it. Or maybe Max tasted like whiskey to start with.

A quick, burning sip; a glimpse of something endless.

Max stood and led me off, away from the bus stop and into the bright asphalt hills of the suburbs. That easy, sheep-ish shuffle, skateboard cradled in the crook of his arm. Sunlight streaming through the tallest trees, leaving shadows of leaves on our cheekbones, my hand in his the entire time. The walk took forever, and we passed the flask back and forth between us as we strolled along. When we were pleas-antly toasted, we took turns saying the alphabet backward and were both surprised at how easy it turned out to be.

That afternoon Max and I pushed deep into unknown suburbs, stumbling along the curb and toying drunkenly with the fringes of front lawns. Even though the neighbor-hoods were unfamiliar, this was a universe that we both understood. We knew which way to go on instinct alone. This was where we had come from. The world of lawns and driveways and tall trees, Tudors and Colonials. And all those driveways were just sliding past us, every one of them another asphalt pathway to someplace familiar and long ago. Every one of them was a story we both knew. We should have followed one of those paths—should have let ourselves pass out in some lady's backyard, face in the dirt. Maybe a small difference like that would have changed something. But we kept on walking until the roads became home again.

When I got back to my house, the sun was gone, and there in the dark, on my lawn, Max kissed me good-bye. This kiss was different from our other kisses. It was tentative and sweet and not at all slobbery. At the time I thought the difference was that he was starting to actually mean it.

"I'll see you around," he said.

"I'll see you," I said.

"Who was that?" my mother asked when I stepped inside. She was sitting on the front staircase, busy polishing the stairs with a rag. She looked crazed, the way she was scrubbing furiously away at just one step.

"Who was who?"

"That guy you were kissing," she said.

"Oh," I said. "That was just Max."

"I see," she said.

"So? What's your point?"

"You smell like alcohol." She narrowed her eyes at me. "Are you drunk?"

"No," I said. "I don't see how you can smell anything with all the Pledge, anyway."

My mom looked unconvinced, but she dropped the subject. I stumbled past her, up the stairs to the bathroom, where I knelt at the toilet, about to be sick. So I was drunk. It didn't matter. Francie and Max had both revealed themselves to me, and now, armed with knowledge, I was stronger than ever. It had been a good day.

Chapter Twenty-three

I was back at the mall, flying solo. It felt good to be by myself. I felt more powerful alone than with Francie; I was finally free from the distraction of her all-consuming needs.

But even though I was stealing more and more, with speed and precision that I had never known, it was not enough. I'd stolen so much, but I'd yet to find the thing I was looking for. My brother was holding on by a thread, time was running out, and with nothing left to trust, I sat at the fountain, waiting for a clue.

The mall had always come through for me before, always at the perfect moment. Francie, Max, even Liz—the mall had given me each of them when I had needed them. That day, waiting for a map I could follow to the Most Beautiful

Thing, I came up with nothing. The mall was showing its stubborn streak. Instead of giving up its secrets, it gave me Max and Francie, both at once.

I saw Francie first. She didn't see me, or maybe she was only pretending not to. She was just milling around, a hundred yards off, looking in windows, fiddling with her hair, listless and bored-looking, a shadow of her former self. She reminded me of me, almost—the way I'd been before I'd met her, in the days when I'd come to the mall alone in the hope of a transformation.

I'd transformed, all right. And so had Francie. I had exceeded my own expectations. Francie had become diminished. I was so wrapped up in watching her that I didn't notice Max sneak up next to me until his hands were covering my eyes. "Guess who," he whispered in my ear. He nibbled on it, sending a shiver up my spine, and I laughed.

"I give up," I said.

When Max took his hands away, he looked so hot—in a worn, white T-shirt, a tiny patch of skin peeking out through a hole over his left breast—that I had to take him somewhere. I stood and looked behind me to see Francie, oblivious to us, examining a pair of sunglasses at Sunglass Hut. So I grabbed Max's hand and led him through the mall, past Sears, to the girls' room and into the handicap stall.

Max had already pulled off of me when she found us there, but it was all perfectly clear anyway. It might as well have been written on the bathroom wall in thick black Sharpie, just to bring it all home.

My blouse was halfway undone; my bra strap was inching down my biceps. Max's face was slick and shiny and newly kiwi-flavored. He was just standing up when the door to the handicap stall busted open.

Max jumped back. I was still on the floor, legs tucked under my knees and wedged between the toilet and the wall. I did not move.

Francie stood there, one fist on her hip, head cocked for action.

"I had a feeling I would find you here," Francie said. She had a certain brightness in her eyes. "I don't know why; I just had a feeling." She tapped a pink press-on claw to her temple. "That old sixth sense. And look! Here you are."

I kept my cool. "Hi," I said. "I thought I locked the door."

I tried to make myself look more respectable without being too obvious about it. But you could never get one past Francie. She rolled her eyes and tossed her hair with vengeful hauteur.

"Please. Go ahead. Put your clothes back on," she said. "I mean, really. What did I expect?" She turned to Max and smiled. "Hi, Max."

The thing is, Francie didn't scare me anymore, even like this. Nothing scared me anymore. I didn't shrink. I looked her straight in the eye and let a certain darkness make its way across my face. "What, exactly, did you expect? Honestly, I'd like to know."

She just raised her chin and folded her arms across her chest.

No one made a move. Max glanced from one of us to the other, unsure and nervous-eyed, and lamenting, almost certainly, the fact that he did not have a joint close at hand. He said nothing. He stood up, pushed past Francie, out of the bathroom stall, and walked away. He moved as if in slow motion, and I watched him go, not saying anything myself but knowing, this time for sure, that if I ever saw him again—which was doubtful—we would both be entirely different people. I wanted to be sad, but there wasn't time.

Francie watched me watch him. For a second, she seemed to cool down. And then we both heard the bathroom door swing closed, a wheeze and a slam.

"You said you didn't want him anyway," I said.

"I don't want him. He's a fucking snake, trust me. That has nothing to do with it."

She didn't have to say it. I knew. "Let me tell you a joke," Francie said.

I let her have her way.

"A blonde and a brunette go to the mall," she said. "The blonde is a total moron and does something typically humiliating and retarded."

"Francie," I said. She barreled on.

"For instance: she eats a turd because she thinks it's chocolate."

"Francie," I said.

"She walks into a glass door and breaks her nose. She actually dares to think that someone is her friend." Francie shrugged and tossed her hair. "Something like that. All laugh."

Francie began to laugh uproariously. I just looked at her.

"You're not laughing," she said. "What? Haven't you ever heard a blonde joke before?"

"I guess you had to be there," I said.

"I guess so," said Francie. "Well. Maybe it's not like funny ha-ha, anyway. But listen. What I want to know, Valentina Martinez, is: Who's the blonde of this joke? Who in this picture is the bimbo and the slut? I am looking for an honest answer here, and I'm starting to wonder if the punch line is maybe precisely as obvious as it first appears."

"Maybe, maybe not," I said. "Personally I've never found blonde jokes funny anyway."

Francie took her eyeliner from her purse and, right there in front of me, applied a new coat, her glare fixed on me the entire time.

"A person can have secrets," I said. "I learned from the master."

"A person can have secrets. But this is something different," Francie said. "We're supposed to be friends. And this is our stall."

"We haven't been in this stall in months," I said.

She slid the tube back into its pocket. "Well?" she prompted me.

"Well what?"

"Aren't you going to say sorry?" she asked. "It's the least you could do."

"No," I said. "I'm not. Because I kissed Max? Why should I apologize to you for that?"

Francie had her hand on her hip. She was still waiting.

"I mean, I guess it must come as a surprise to you," I continued. "I guess it must come as a surprise that someone would choose me over you. You thought you could just drag me along with you, just keep me to prop you up. I wonder if it ever occurred to you that I could be anything more than your partner in crime."

Francie's face fell. "I can't believe you would say that," she said.

"Oh really?"

"You actually think that?"

I didn't answer her. Why bother? "I'm leaving," I said. And I did.

Max was nothing if not a creature of unparticular urges. Given a path, he would follow it. And given any deterrent whatsoever, he would bail on a dime. That was just Max. I knew him well enough to know. The easy smirk; the constantly shifting gaze. Those long, awkward arms and legs; the eager, skittish soul of a dog. It wasn't too hard to figure him out, in the end.

Francie, though. Francie was more of a mystery.

Because that night, the same day she'd caught me in the bathroom with Max, she called me. "I'm sorry," she said.

"What do you mean?" I asked. "I mean, why are you apologizing?"

"You're allowed to have a life," she said. "I told you I didn't want Max. And if I'm not going to have him, why shouldn't you? It would be a legitimate waste. I just wish you hadn't kept it secret. You didn't have to do that, and anyway, it's not like I didn't suspect. You could have told me. I wouldn't have been mad. And I'm not mad. I understand."

"Well, it doesn't matter now," I said.

"I shouldn't have said the stuff I said the other day, either," she said. "I don't know why I said it. I was just frustrated. But we'll find it, babe."

"What stuff? Find what?" I asked.

"The Holy Grail," she said. "All that stuff. I know it's important to you. I will not let you down. Have I ever let you down?"

"Okay," I said lamely. I didn't even really know what I was agreeing with.

"Good. Then it's all good," Francie said.

There was nothing I could do. Ever since the day we'd kissed in the girls' room, Francie had a hold over me. I had tried my hardest to let her go. It would not work.

"It's all good," I said.

"Great, babe. We'll go to the mall tomorrow. Bring your rubber bands!"

At Montgomery Shoppingtowne the next day, I let Francie flutter at my side again. At first I barely noticed she was even there. She stole with lackluster gracelesseness, just dropping stuff in her bag without bothering to disguise herself with the usual plumage. She was wearing a gray, ill-fitting sweatshirt and a pair of jeans that made her butt look kind of big. Clunky New Balance sneakers that squeaked when she walked. When I pointed out that she had only put her eyeliner on one eye, she just dropped a package of bath beads in her purse and shrugged. "It's avant-garde," she said, but it sounded like an excuse.

And maybe it was the disbelieving way I rolled my eyes, or maybe she was drawing one last bit of energy from the bath beads she'd just taken. Whatever it was, she willed something to return to her.

She went off to the bathroom, and when she came back it was just like the other week at the Gap, except more. She had cloaked herself again in dazzle. Heels and hair and big, barely hidden tits. She was wearing the exact outfit she had worn on the first day of school. Hot pants and skimpy tube top with gold lace-up sandals. She was shining. This time, though, I knew it was just an illusion—one of the last tricks she had in her arsenal. I didn't bother to be impressed.

"Well?" she grilled me. "Better?"

I didn't feel like humoring her. "I guess," I said.

Her face fell, and for a moment she began to wane, but then she collected herself. She took my arm in hers and dragged me out into the mall. "Come on," she said. "Let's find it. Today's the day. I can feel it in my bones! I mean, isn't there something about today? Can't you tell that we're on the trail of it? Can't you feel that everything is about to get better?"

"It's not exactly breezy in here," I said. But I wanted to believe her. I wanted to believe *in* her. If nothing else, I guess, I wanted to believe in the mall. I was still looking for it myself, so why not give Francie one last chance? Maybe the mall had returned her for a reason.

"Sure," I said. "Lead the way, you hot bitch."

Francie beamed. That was all it took for her to sweep me right back up in her enthusiasm. She still had that power over me. We were bound together whether I liked it or not.

So Francie pointed straight ahead and used her finger as a divining rod. Her hand swayed back and forth, up and down in the air, before finally settling on a store. Spencer Gifts. And a kind of faith started to swell in my chest. Spencer's—it was the last place in the entire universe that you would expect to find an ancient, holy artifact. Which meant that maybe we were on the right track.

We went to Spencer's, and Francie made a big show of doing her eyeliner just so, of snapping the rubber bands around her wrists, tossing her hair and shaking it out before stepping through the entranceway.

In the store no one paid attention to us. It wasn't any kind of trickery or technique on our part, it was just that we weren't really worth paying attention to.

So we walked in unnoticed, and Francie made her way around the tightly packed store, eyeing things carefully, picking them up and examining them, smelling them, while I trailed along. She was making a real show out of it.

"I can feel it. It's here," Francie said. "It's calling to me, I'm legitimately sure of it. Valentina Martinez, this is going to change everything. The Holy Grail. The one thing that has eluded us."

The store was full of the dumbest stuff imaginable. I mean, that's the point of Spencer's; it's stuff only a little brother or a gym teacher would find funny. For instance, a naked lady pencil sharpener where the pencil was intended to be inserted just where you would imagine. Francie picked it up and pondered it, then rolled her eyes. "I don't think so," she said, and she dropped it in her purse anyway. "I'll give it to Dan for his birthday," she said. "He'll think it's hilarious."

We examined a board game for sexually bored "married couples," a pair of velvet-lined handcuffs, a remote-controlled fart machine, and several black lights of various size and price. Francie was unimpressed by all of it, like any sensible person would be, and as her search continued, she got more and more manic, fidgeting with her hair and shimmying her hips and snapping her fingers distractedly.

And then, in the back corner of the store, she was shaking an eighty-dollar pole dancer kit at her ear when her head jerked up. Francie's eyes sparkled with her earrings, and briefly I thought she was about to transform. But she didn't; she had just spotted something else that caught her interest.

"Val," she whispered stagily. "There it is."

I caught my breath, full of unexpected anticipation. I turned and followed her gaze to a giant, heavy plastic beer cup that was shaped like a cowboy boot. "I told you," she said. She took the boot off the shelf and caressed it, her boobs heaving excitedly under her tube top. "I told you it would be something that seemed just normal at first. Something that startled you with how beautiful it was. And don't you see?"

It was just a big, hollow hunk of molded plastic. My mouth tightened. "Pretty beautiful, all right," I said through gritted teeth.

If Francie sensed my rage, she couldn't see it yet. "Not just beautiful," she breathed. "The *most* beautiful. The Most Beautiful Thing."

I searched her face. She was looking up at me with desperate, crazed hopefulness, the beer boot clutched tightly to her chest, the rings of gold around her pupils pulsating. I just shook my head.

Francie bit her lip and smiled wider. She looked almost

terrified. Like she knew that this was her last chance. And I knew it was bitchy of me. I owed her so much. But our friendship had been built on more than one promise, and one of the promises—in some ways the most important one—had been that she was better than this.

Seeing her like that, I knew that I had been lied to. The way she had toyed with the one thing that was still important to me, thinking she could sink her claws deeper.

"It's getting late," I said, checking the time on my phone. "I gotta go." I turned and left her standing there. "I'm sorry," I said as I walked away. But I wasn't actually sorry. I looked back over my shoulder and I could barely stomach the sight of her. She was teetering on her heels, knife-thin stilettos that could no longer support the overwhelming weight of her ambition. And then the heels crumbled. The eyeliner melted away. Francie's lips were thin and dull, her hair tangled and limp and in desperate need of a new dye job. Her eyes were wide and pleading. Francie in baggy, big-butt jeans and a gray, ill-fitting sweatshirt. She had that boot clutched tight to her breasts, like if she hugged it close enough, she could swallow it inside her body and absorb its fake-o fucking magic.

Francie had never been anything without me, and she had known it all along. She would not let me go. She was a vampire. In order to save myself, you can see, destroying her was my only choice.

Chapter Twenty-four

It was June, the twilight bit of not-quite-summer when everything is in between—either coming or going. My hair had grown out since the day Francie had cut it all off in her bathroom. I was someone different now. After the day in Spencer Gifts, I had stolen a bottle of Clairol Pure White from CVS. Now I was the type of girl who didn't need a name.

You know the type I'm talking about: Blond. Big boobs. Total slut. The kind of girl who, when you heard people in the halls talking about "*her,*" you didn't question for a second who it was that they were actually talking about. They were talking about *her.* They were talking about me.

When it comes to that kind of girl—the kind of girl who doesn't need a name, the kind of girl who was me—the requirements are loose. Maybe certain criteria are not exactly set in stone. It's a *type*, but there are variations. There are misinterpretations. For instance, it's possible that people just *think* she's a slut, even though she's never actually gotten down with anyone at all. Maybe her boobs are really not all that giant, it's just that she *acts* like they are. With the tube tops and everything.

One point, however, is not up for negotiation: she's always the blonde. Even if she doesn't start as a blonde, she'll end up that way soon enough—trust me. I was a blonde now. Certain things will turn your hair gold.

I didn't need a name anymore, but Francie didn't have one. No one bothered to talk about her anymore. When you heard people talking about the slutty bitch who thought she was too good for everyone else, they were probably talking about me. It was as if Francie had never existed at all. Except she had existed. I remembered her.

I still even saw her sometimes. I think I must have been the only one. When she walked down the hall that June, no one bothered to stare. She was shoulder-to-locker, her blond hair unwashed and unstyled, flat and dull and kind of growing into brown. She had a shell-shocked look in her eyes.

And one day I was heading to my locker in a red stretch minidress with matching heels and a tangle of gold chains around my neck, with my hair piled in a shining tower, when I felt a firm grip on my arm.

I twisted. It was Mrs. O'Keefe, the vice principal.

"Excuse me!" I snapped and tried to pull away. But she had a grip of steel. She narrowed her eyes and pulled something green and vinyl from behind her back.

"Skirt's so short you need *two* haircuts," she growled, and handed over the raincoat. "Put it on," she said. I laughed in her face, not even trying to be rude, but just because I truly thought it was funny.

Later that day I was coming out of the bathroom, still wearing the Whore's Raincoat with pride, when I saw Francie slumped against a locker. She looked up at me like she'd been waiting, and I tried to bolt but couldn't. It was too late; she had locked me in her gaze. A flicker of a smile played at the corners of her lips. She seemed almost amused at my outfit.

I did not smile. I let my eyes bore into her skull, straight through to the locker behind her. I let black inky tendrils crawl from my body and wrap around her. I willed her to disappear as she faded, faded. I didn't breathe until she was gone.

I thought I had obliterated her.

Chapter Twenty-five

There is an afternoon that I don't remember much about. I wonder if it will always be lost, or if someday I will recall the specifics of exactly what happened. I wonder, but then again, I suppose I would rather just let it all go.

The things I do remember about that afternoon are, for various reasons, mostly inconsequential. I remember, of course, what I was wearing: a plain black shirtdress, black tights, red flats, and, in my hair, a red ribbon. I remember I was watching Judge Judy on television and she was yelling at the plaintiff because he could not produce receipts. Judge Judy was saying, "You claim to have the proof, sir, but where is the pudding? Where is the pudding?"

I remember the weather. I hadn't been outside that day,

but I remember looking out the window and seeing the day and thinking it was beautiful.

The one other thing I remember about that afternoon would be significant except for the fact that it can't have actually happened. And something that didn't happen can't be important. Can it?

Decide for yourself. Judge Judy was screeching and screeching and it was starting to make me feel kind of nauseated, so I turned off the television, and then there was a knock at my door. It was Jesse. I knew why he had come.

I should have been shocked to see him, but I wasn't. It seemed natural and ordinary that he should appear just then. It's only polite to say good-bye. He was standing at the threshold, holding a big cardboard box.

"Hey there, big brother," I said. I didn't make a move toward him, and he didn't step any farther into my bedroom, just dropped the box at his feet. A groan and a thud. It was my brother, but this return was not like any of his previous ones. He wasn't the same anymore; his smile was happy and full of the future, unmitigated by artifice or apology.

"Hey, Blondie," he said. "Looking good."

I touched my hair.

"Thanks. What's in the box?"

"Just some stuff I wanted to return to you."

"Oh."

"You're going to be on your own now," he said. "But I think you'll be okay."

I had to laugh, even though it was not the time or place. "I'll be okay? I'll be on my own? Like I'm not already on my own? Who has ever taken care of me? You? I see you, like, once every million days."

"It's true."

"Whatever," I said. I was annoyed with him, knowing exactly how inappropriate it was to feel that way at that moment.

"Don't be like that," Jesse said. "What's the point of being like that now?" We looked at each other. Jesse ran his fingers through his hair. Left hand, right hand. And then I wasn't annoyed anymore, because I just wanted him to stay. I thought maybe if I just kept talking and talking forever, I could trap him there, on the threshold of my bedroom.

"You wouldn't believe everything that's been going on," I said. "I got an F on my History test, and Mr. Fogelman told me that he thought I should visit the school psychologist, which is like the most insane thing I ever heard, so I told him that if he tried to flunk me, I was going to tell everyone—"

"I can't talk," Jesse cut me off. "I wasn't even supposed to come here at all. I just wanted to return this stuff. So . . ."

"Stay," I said.

He shrugged, smiled, and gave me a half wave, which was really more like a flick of the wrist, then turned to go before thinking better of it and turning back. "You'll be fine," he said. "I'm proud of you. Look at you. Look at what you've become. I mean, really. A blonde? You're blonder than blond.

You are harder than diamond. You could survive anything."
He winked, and I knew that now that he was dead he could
see everything, in all tenses, as an uncomplicated panorama.
I knew that he knew exactly what I had become. He wasn't
trying to give me a compliment.

"Jesse," I said.

He turned and went.

"Come back," I said. And all I wanted was for him to
look at me one last time. He did not. All I wanted was for
him to turn around and say something—anything—that
would give me a clue to where I was going, or what I was
supposed to do next. All I wanted was for him to forgive me.

He did not.

When he was gone, I knelt on the floor and opened up
the box he'd left behind, and in it were all the things that
Francie and I had stolen for him. Here were the books, the
underwear, the T-shirts and baseball caps and action figures
and scented candles—all of it, every useless talisman. I was
surprised that it all fit in one box. It seemed like there
should have been more. But it was definitely everything.

I wondered why he'd felt the need to return the stuff to
me. It had all been a gift; it was never meant to be returned.
But maybe he believed in things that were stolen, believed
they had a purpose in the larger plan of the world, and that
somehow I was part of that plan, too.

Maybe. Or maybe he just couldn't travel to his next
Elsewhere with all that shit weighing him down.

It doesn't matter. I know none of this is possible. I know it didn't happen. I had believed in a lot of stupid things, and I'd finally learned my lesson. If there's one thing I don't believe in, it's ghosts.

What I do and do not choose to believe in, however, does not change the fact that the box of stuff was in my bedroom. I don't believe in ghosts. But it got there somehow.

When my cell rang, I didn't need to look at the display to know who it was. It was Liz.

"Hey," she said. "I've got bad news and bad news."

I don't remember what I said.

I wished I was fearless. Harder than diamond.

I wished I knew a person who could change things. Someone with special abilities, special sight. Someone with force of will so overpowering that all she had to do was want something and it would be hers. Just like that. Someone who didn't make promises she couldn't keep, whose bite was worse than her bark, whose bra was not stuffed with silicone falsies her mom had ordered for her off QVC.

I didn't know anyone like that. But I wished I did. I was not that kind of person. I wasn't sure if I wished I was or not.

My brother was dead and then it was dark out. I don't know what time it was. Maybe early, maybe late, but either way dark. My mother was downstairs somewhere, planning things with Jack. I was in my bedroom, with all the lights off, sitting on the floor in a corner. I thought about calling Max, but I knew he wouldn't remember me. I thought about calling Francie, but I knew it was too late for that.

Certain things are open to interpretation. And other things are pretty incontrovertible, even if you would rather not admit it. Here are some facts: Jesse had gone. Max had gone. Liz was leaving. And as for Francie. Well. I was alone.

I thought about going to the mall. But the mall was no place for me anymore.

Chapter Twenty-six

The afternoon after Jesse died, I snuck out of my bedroom, still in my pajamas, and into the room that had once been his. Jesse's room had floundered in disuse since he'd left for college, the door inching open only when my mom was on a cleaning kick or on the incredibly rare occasions when he himself had chosen to grace us with his presence. Now he was dead. The day after Jesse died, I eased the door open with no idea what it would be like to be in there now that it had no owner at all. I was prepared to cry, or puke, or have a fainting spell. But when I stepped inside and looked around, none of those things happened. I felt fine.

Jesse's room had not changed at all. In there he would be seventeen forever, except when he was twelve, or ten, or six. The more closely you looked, the younger he got. Sure, the wall was all plastered with posters of Nirvana and the Ramones and Scotch-taped pictures of Liz shoving her tongue between four spread fingers. And there was that ancient, dog-eared copy of *Freshmen* in the desk drawer under a red spiral notebook. But then you scanned down the bookshelf only to find row after row of Hardy Boys books, and, lower, two plastic milk crates brimming with at least one hundred He-Man action figures. A threadbare, nameless old teddy bear on the bed, flung carelessly across the pillow. The cheesy, framed needlepoint on the wall proclaiming the day of his birth. My brother had once been very young.

I looked around the room, and Jesse visited me again, one final time. I mean, really, I know that it wasn't him at all. I was just a memory, but it did almost feel as if he was speaking to me. "Fearless," I heard him saying. "You are, like, so fearless." I tried to be brave.

I dialed her number. It wasn't a conscious decision; it was just a muscle memory. A sequence of familiar twitches. I didn't know what I was doing. I didn't want to do it. I just did it. I picked up the old plastic *Sports Illustrated* football phone on Jesse's bedside table, the one he'd been given as a joke on some birthday or another, and dialed her number. I didn't even know if she would still exist to answer. But she did.

"Hey, bitch," she answered. Like nothing had changed. Francie still held the ability to astonish with her willful obliviousness.

"Hey, bitch," I said.

"You weren't in school today," she said.

"I'm going to be out tomorrow, too," I told her. That was all I had to say. Despite everything, it still worked that way between us.

"Your brother died?" she asked.

"Yep."

"That sucks. Does it suck?"

"I don't know," I said. "It's not like a surprise or anything."

"I have an English test tomorrow," she offered.

"That sucks, too," I said. I was feeling ghoulish, there on Jesse's old bed. I twirled the cord around my finger and imagined him doing it, in that exact pose.

Francie's voice was tough and throaty in my ear as I sat on Jesse's bed. I was barely listening.

The room was starting to overwhelm me. I wondered if my mom was going to do that thing where she'd leave it untouched forever, like some weird museum. That's what they always do on TV when a kid dies, but I didn't figure my mother for the type. She was too into decorating and home improvement. It was pretty amazing that she'd left it alone for as long as she had. I figured as soon as the funeral was over, she'd probably spend a year stripping the paint on the windows and refinishing the floors, and then turn the room into a study for Jack or something.

"We'll go to the mall," Francie's voice was echoing through the cheap plastic of the phone. "You'll feel better."

"Now?" I asked, still sort of disoriented.

"No. Tomorrow. I'll skip. That way you won't have to sit around the house all day with your mom. She must be going totally crazy, huh?"

"Skip? You sure?" I asked. "Didn't you skip your last English test, too?"

"That was, like, three tests ago. Anyway, for you, baby, I'll skip another. I haven't read stupid *Midsummer Night's Whatever*, so it's not like it matters. A girl spends her summer reading every tragedy Shakespeare ever wrote, and they go ahead and assign a comedy. So predictable."

"Well, you're not missing much," I said. "My class read it last quarter. In the end nothing happened."

"I had a feeling it might turn out that way," she said.

I hung up and went downstairs to see what my mother was up to. She was in the living room with a vacuum cleaner, vacuuming the couch, looking as happy as I ever remembered her being. She had pushed all the furniture to the corners of the living room, and was dressed in her cleaning outfit: an old checked blouse and a pair of baggy jeans, a hot-pink Minnie Mouse bandanna on her head.

"Don't you have better things to be doing?" I asked.

"What'd you say?" my mom shouted over the roar of the vacuum before realizing that it would be clever to shut it off.

"I said, don't you have better things to be doing? For instance, crying or something?"

"It's funny," she said. "I haven't felt like it yet. I tried last night, and it just would not come. At first I felt guilty, but then I remembered that Oprah Winfrey says everyone mourns differently. I suppose I'll cry sooner or later. Maybe I'll be one of those people who throws myself in the grave at the funeral. You never know."

"They say vacuuming is the first stage of grief," I said.

"Come on. It's not like we haven't been expecting it. In a way, it's a relief. I know that's a horrible thing to say, but it's true."

"It's still horrible," I said.

My mother finally looked like she might actually be sad. "I know," she said. "I've been a horrible mother. Even worse to you than to him. I'm sorry." She stretched out her arms to me and beckoned me in for a hug. I ignored her.

"Francie's sleeping over," I said.

My mother didn't drop her arms. "Fine with me," she said. "Just don't make a mess." I left my mother standing with her arms outstretched like she was some B-movie zombie. I called Francie back.

"Will you sleep over?"

"I'll have to sneak out," she said. "Just because my mom's an alcoholic and a lunatic doesn't mean she'll let me sleep over on a Wednesday night."

"Obviously you tell her Jesse died," I told her.

"You got the hang of that pretty quickly," Francie said. "How long are you gonna use it to keep yourself out of school?"

"How long do you think I can get away with it?"

"A week. Two, tops."

"School will be over in two weeks. Fuck exams."

Francie arrived on my doorstep an hour later in a tight hot-pink cocktail dress with white polka dots and big, poofy, off-the-shoulder sleeves. She was wearing enormous sunglasses and a black and floppy wide-brimmed hat.

"Hey," I said when I answered the door. It was a relief to see her this way. I decided to pretend that the last few months had only been a dream. "I like the dress," I said.

Francie giggled. "It's my mom's," she said. "She wore it to some wedding, like, a trillion years ago, and I borrowed it. I threw out most of my own clothes"—she paused, searching for the best way to put it, then soldiered on—"you know. A while ago. I decided to streamline. I'm becoming an ascetic. But I figured on a day like today I needed to wear something a little bit glamorous. Out of respect for your dead brother and all."

Francie was still standing on the doorstep, as if she was unsure whether to come inside. "It's perfect," I said. And I stepped back and beckoned her inside, and we both hovered around each other in the foyer, circling, before I finally stood up on my tiptoes and threw my arms around my best friend's neck. She hugged me back. "You are too good," she murmured. "Babe, you are too good for words."

"Wanna play MASH?" I asked, squeezing tighter.

"Fuck yes," Francie said, gasping for air. "My future could always use some illumination."

So we went down to the basement, where I found a piece of scrap paper and read Francie's fortune in a spiral. Dwelling: apartment. Transportation: roller skates. Husband: Morrissey. Secret destiny: immortality. Then she flipped the paper over and did mine.

That night, my brother's room was still calling to us. All those mysterious drawers and crevices and old envelopes stuffed with gross letters from various skanky guys—the dark places that had always been off-limits to a sister—were now mine by rights. Jesse was gone and it felt like all the doors had been flung open.

"A dead man can't object to snooping," Francie said as she pulled a long-forgotten bag of weed out from behind a book on the shelf. "It is, in fact, our solemn duty." We smoked the pot, not even worrying about anyone smelling it, and went to sleep early in Jesse's old bed.

In Jesse's bed that night, Francie gripped me tight as we fell asleep, both of us still a little bit stoned. Her skinny arms around my waist, her smallish breasts against mine, and her knees tucked snug against her belly. Without the high heels and the towering ponytail and the falsies, she was actually very little.

That night, I was drifting off when she grabbed my wrists and started shaking. Like a blade of grass or a tiny bug. My brother was dead and Francie was just the softest buzz in my ear. "I knew you weren't gone for good," she whispered. "I knew you always had my back; I never had a stitch of doubt."

I pretended to be asleep. Francie kept talking, rambling drowsily. "You could never leave me, babe. We're sisters. We have come too far. I will never let you go again."

And please imagine the following in pink ballpoint pen. With bubbles to dot the *i*'s except that there are no *i*'s. Please imagine the following in tight, bouncy script, with letters crammed tight and edge to edge like there is a shortage of paper, except there's plenty. This is my handwriting. I have always had excellent penmanship.

Here is the last item in that tiny leather notebook. You thought it was already over, but you were wrong. Here it is: The End. *We went to the mall.*

Chapter Twenty-seven

Francie and I woke just before noon and got dressed together. We huddled at the bathroom mirror deep in concentration as we both did our eyeliner. I teased my hair into a giant tangled tower and set it in place with a can of Aqua Net. Skintight black jeans tucked into knee-high stiletto Nine West boots, lipstick overripe plum.

When I zipped my motorcycle jacket all the way up to my chin, Francie looked at me and whistled. "Just . . . wow," she said. "Did I tell you yet how good you look as a blonde?"

Francie was wearing the same outfit she'd had on yesterday. The hat, the sunglasses, the ancient cocktail dress. It was Francie, for sure. We hopped on the bus and took the trip one final time. When we arrived at the mall, we climbed onto the sidewalk, and Francie put her hand on my shoulder, and there was a breeze. We stood together, our hair shel-lacked in place a foot above each of our heads, both staring up at the structure above us.

I had changed. Francie had changed. Almost everything had changed, in one way or another. In the end, you are always older. But the mall had not changed. The mall would never change. The mall was all things at all times. It was a secret and a hope and a suspicion. It was a graveyard and a ghost town. Above all, it was a persistence. All that time Francie and I had thought we were stealing from it, when really it was taking what it wanted from us. My brother was gone.

The mall had already succeeded in pushing itself into the future; now it had set its sights on moving outward, and beyond.

We went to the Gap first. I wanted to say good-bye to Liz. In fact, I was worried that she had already heeded the call of the koalas.

She hadn't. She was standing behind the counter, drum-ming her fingers and breathing down the neck of the clerk at the cash register. The bright halogen light bounced from the clean, shiny cedar floors and columns, lending everything a harsh white glare. Liz had her hair in a businesslike French braid and wore a prissy silk scarf tied around her neck. You know the type of scarf I mean. The type an English teacher would pair with a jeweled ladybug pin on the breast pocket of her red blazer.

"Hey, Liz," I said. "You look fancy."

"Hi, Valentina," Liz said. "Hi, Francie." She smiled, but

it wasn't her usual smile. Her lips were cherry red, matte, and lined in maroon. She had lipstick on her teeth.

"I just came to say good-bye. You said there wouldn't be time, but I thought I'd, you know, try or whatever."

"Thanks," Liz said. "That's so nice of you. It really is nice." She hadn't made a move. She seemed distracted by the girl at the register. "Crystal," she said to the girl, "you have to press CANCEL before you enter your register number again."

"So," I said. Francie was swiveling her head back and forth between me and Liz with a funny, perplexed expression. "So when are you leaving?" I asked.

Liz took a deep breath. The whole time we had been talking, she had not stopped drumming her nails. Rat-a-tat-tat, rat-a-tat-tat. Crystal was growing increasingly frustrated at her task, jamming the same button over and over only to be met with a long, annoying beep. "Here's the thing, Valentina," Liz said. She reached over and turned the key on the register to shut it off. "Go fold some shirts, Crystal," she said, and the girl stalked off, all disgruntled. Liz turned back to us. "Here's the thing. I'm not leaving. They offered me general manager. This morning. My own store. An offer I can't, like, refuse. This whole place is mine now." She drew her hand over her head in a rainbow like she expected me to be impressed. And I almost was.

Francie wasn't having it. It was almost disturbing how my brother's death seemed to have resurrected the old Francie. "It was always yours," she said. "I thought that's what we were always saying all along."

Liz pretended she hadn't even heard her. "Listen," Liz said. "I'm going to have to ask you guys not to come back here. We can still be friends and all, but it's not, like, fun and games anymore. The bottom line's my business now. I can't have all the . . ." She trailed off. "You know. The thing is, I think maybe it's time for all of us to grow up. Better to do it before it's too late."

"Come on," Francie said. I followed her as she stalked out of the store. I tried to wave good-bye to Liz, but she had already turned her attention elsewhere.

"I cannot fucking believe her," Francie said when we were clear. "The hypocrisy!"

"I can't blame her," I said. "Everyone has their own crap to deal with. You can't judge a person for the way she handles it."

Francie stole a lot of shit that day. It was indisputable that she had gotten her magic back. I didn't even know she was taking anything, and then we'd leave the store and she would have something new in her bag. She stole bras and bras and bras from Intimates at Bloomingdale's, and a huge stack of DVDs from FYE. She stole flip-flops and a bathing suit from PacSun, and Satsuma scented soap from the Body Shop, and three pairs of sunglasses from the rack at Anthropologie. She stole a handful of thongs with Hostess cupcakes on the crotch from Hot Topic, and sweatpants that said DADDY'S L'IL GIRL across the butt from Fashion Dump. And on and on and on and on, and only warming up.

I didn't bother taking anything. There was nothing I wanted.

We went to Abercrombie & Fitch, to the underwear wall. "For my future husband, Morrissey," Francie said. "Do you think he likes boxer-briefs, or brief-briefs?"

"I can't see Morrissey in boxer-briefs," I said.

"Brief-briefs, then. Regular or low-rise?"

"I don't know?"

"I'm going to go with low-rise. I like when you can see just a hint of pube."

She was working her charms on rows of undies, but I just looked at the pictures. I looked at the packages in front of me. The posters on the wall. These headless men with their smoothly etched muscles and tiny, flinty nipples. Hairless and big-chested enough to be women, except that they weren't. Maybe they were from a different universe, I thought. A more hearty universe where there was no such thing as a man or a woman, just these freaks in their underpants who were kind of both and kind of neither. And no need for the mess or the hassle or disease. They could just be in love with themselves. They reminded me of Francie.

My brother was gone. After every other thing had fallen away, I'd still held out hope that I could keep him, and I had failed.

Francie had somehow regained herself that day, and I felt

like I was waning in her presence. I mean, I guess I deserved it, but still.

"Let's go to Claire's," Francie suggested.

At Claire's, Francie occupied herself with the new stuff on the racks while I perused the bins of half-priced trinkets out of boredom, and that was when I found it, without even really looking. When I say *it*, I think you know what I mean.

I was digging through spray-paint-gilded bangles when it caught my eye from the next bin over. It was a sparkle that cut through the dull shimmer of junky baubles and glittery plastic crap. It jumped out at me, shot its spark right to the periphery of my vision, and I didn't even have to turn my head to know. There it was.

It was the Most Beautiful Thing. It was what we had been looking for all along. The Holy Grail.

I held my breath, terrified that something would go wrong. But it was right there. No one could stop me, and I reached out and took it. It almost burned my hand, but I took it and clutched it in my fist and shoved my fist in my jacket pocket. I played with the thing as we left the store, rolled it over in my fingers, feeling its heat, its heft, the way it seemed to change shape as I twisted it. I squeezed it so hard that I was afraid I might draw blood.

"Well, that was a bust," Francie said when we were out. "I feel like I already have ten of everything at Claire's."

Francie had always believed in unbelievable things. She had opened up a door that had led me to this dream-mall, a place where everything—every single thing—was just sitting there, waiting to be stolen. Francie had been right all along. The Holy Grail had been under our noses this whole time. But I had found it too late. What good was it going to do me now?

I toyed with it, thinking how stupid it all was. I thought about the many ways I had failed everyone.

Then we were caught.

Francie was the one who was blindsided, not me. With the Most Beautiful Thing in my hand I had a kind of second sight, and I saw mall security before they even rounded the corner, aiming for us in sharky strides. I caught my breath and looked over at her, and she seemed, in that glance, so unimpressive. Even with two bags full of loot, even in her enormous hat.

Francie had chosen me for a reason. In Ms. Tinker's Physics class, where foolishness went explicitly against policy, Francie had foolishly thought that I could protect her. It turned out it hadn't been so foolish after all, though, because she was right. I could.

Security was heading for us, and I floated outside myself, looking down from above, able to see clearly in every direction and every dimension. There it all was, in chalky, glowing pastel, laid right out in simple geometric shapes. The map of the mall. The map of the world.

Francie had been right all along. I could protect her. I could see it. There were several ways I could have saved her. I saw it unfold exactly as it could happen.

I could have dragged her straight back into Bloomingdale's—only a few feet away—where it would have been easy for us to hide in Furnishings, chest to chest inside an armoire until the coast was clear and we could go about our business.

I could have held her hand in mine and made a dash for it, straight for the narrow, hidden hallway that only we knew about, the one that led to the Q section of the garage. We would have made it easily.

I could have told her to give me her bags, the way she'd done for me long ago at Sephora. Could have stayed there, bags in hand, and told her to get the hell out of there, that I would meet her at the J-12 in twenty-five minutes. She wouldn't have done it, but I could've offered, and it still would have changed certain things.

Or. I could have taken her by the elbow and hustled her into the Gap, where Liz would have sighed and sputtered and rolled her eyes in disapproval, and quickly, without further argument, would have pushed us into the stockroom, where the emergency exit would have taken us right out into the parking lot and safety and back to Francie's house, where we would lie in her bed laughing about our near capture. Smoking cigarettes, her hand on my hip, my brother all but forgotten.

I did not do any of those things. Any one of them would have been a solution in its own way. But I still remembered what she had whispered in my ear, in my bed the night before, when she'd thought I was asleep. *I will never let you go again.*

So I chose to distract her. "You got a shitload of stuff," I said. "It's gotta be your best haul ever, huh?"

I could feel the guards getting closer. I knew that if I didn't keep her off her game she would be able to feel them coming, too. At that moment, she was as good as she had ever been.

"I'm not sure," she said. "We've had some damn good days in the past, you know?"

"True," I said, searching for something else to say. "Did you get any dishes? My mom told me she needs some dishes."

Francie didn't have time to answer. They were on us. She never saw it coming.

And I was not scared. I could hardly remember what being scared felt like. I knew the thing in my pocket would protect me as long as I kept it in my fist. I was cool and unflappable when we were collared by the guards, a fat old man with a cartoonish comb-over and a rail-thin black woman who towered over even Francie in her heels. "Come this way," the woman ordered in a bored monotone.

Francie's head snapped in my direction as they swept us up. Her mascara'd lashes were stunned and spidery; her lips were petrified in a half kiss. She knew exactly what I had done. It was all there in that look. Her hand began to flutter toward her face, and I thought for a second she was going to make the Sign, to call for help. But her fingers never made it to her earlobe. She knew that help was not coming; she knew that in order for something like that to work, you have to first believe in it. Francie didn't believe in anything. I wanted her to make a break for it, for her to just drop her bags and let her stilettos carry her away, but I knew that it was too late. She was already broken.

I had no regrets.

Security led us past the Gap, where I could sense Liz's eyes following us, and down the escalator past the fountain, through the food court, and down a narrow hallway behind the childcare room, to a big metal door marked PRIVATE. The whole time, Francie did not say a word. When I looked at her out of the corner of my eye, I saw that she was destroyed. She was breathing heavy, cheeks flushed, spine hunched, and face crumpled.

I'm sure you're wondering why I did it. My answer is complicated. There are so many reasons, after all. Reasons that don't make sense, that argue with each other, that don't add up. But I guess the simplest way of putting it is that I wanted her to understand how she had failed me and Jesse. How she had failed herself. By being ordinary. She was just a regular girl—one who, if you want the whole entire truth, looked completely ridiculous in all that makeup, the miniskirts, the heels, the hair. All she'd ever had was one pointless gift, that illusory, white-hot dazzle. She had never accomplished much with it, and now, when it could have been useful, it would not come to her. Of course it wouldn't come to her.

We were taken to a back office, where the guards left us to

a hulking, dark-haired guy in a threadbare Men's Warehouse suit. I sat, calm, at the conference table, next to Francie, and the guy, whose name tag read MR. GROSSMAN, dumped all her stuff out and glowered at us. "Look what we have here," Mr. Grossman said. "Did you girls pay for any of this?"

"This has nothing to do with me," I said.

"What about you?" Mr. Grossman asked Francie.

"Yes," Francie mumbled. "It's mine. I paid for it."

"What would you say if I told you we had it all on tape?" he asked.

Francie was stoic, but I knew what she was thinking. She was thinking that she knew her angles, knew that there was no way she could have been caught on camera. Mr. Grossman picked up a remote control, and rolled a tape on a monitor, and there she was. Francie in Bloomingdale's, Francie in FYE, PacSun, Abercrombie, and the rest. The cameras had caught everything. Francie's jaw went slack.

Through all of this, my hand had never left my pocket. The thing I held in there was icy and perfect. It was the thing I had been looking for. Even though I no longer had a use for it, I would not let them take it away from me.

"Let's do a little arithmetic," Mr. Grossman said. He had an old-fashioned adding machine on the conference table, and he began to total up Francie's spoils, a piece at a time, *crunch-crunch-crunch-crunch-crunch.* He was making a big production out of it; it was probably the most fun he'd had in months.

"Daddy's L'il Girl sweatpants . . . forty-nine fifty," he said to himself as he entered the figure. He totaled it, *crunch*, and he raised his eyebrows and looked up at Francie. "You know, over five hundred is a felony," he said.

"I've heard that," Francie mumbled. "What are we at so far?"

"Three hundred fifty-nine fifty," he said. I detected a note of glee in his voice. "And we've still got the whole other bag to go!"

I sat there patiently through it all. I didn't have to stay. No one had seen me take the thing in my pocket, and Mr. Grossman didn't seem to suspect. I figured I could leave anytime I wanted to. But I didn't want to.

"*H.R. Pufnstuf* DVD set," Mr. Grossman was droning on. "Tinker Bell car ornament. Low-rise briefs. Someone's got a boyfriend, I guess." I half expected a petulant retort from Francie, but she no longer had it in her. Mr. Grossman kept on going with his tabulation, chuckling here and there at items that he found particularly silly. Finally he was done. I held my breath, waiting. "Four hundred ninety-eight dollars and thirty-one cents," he sighed. "Right under the wire. Lucky for you, missy."

Francie betrayed no relief. She didn't move. Me, though—I started gathering up my things.

This was it. I have to say that I was disappointed. Francie had pulled out one last rip-off. She had won, fair and square; the only punishment she would face having her Polaroid posted in the security office of Montgomery Shoppingtowne, an empty symbol of eternal banishment.

There was really nothing left to see, I figured.

"Can I leave?" I asked.

"I don't know about that," Mr. Grossman said. But I stood anyway, and turned to walk out. No one stopped me. Francie didn't even look up. "We're going to have to take your Polaroid, for the wall," Mr. Grossman told her.

I was angry. I had always been angry. But there are worse things to be than angry.

As angry as I was, I wasn't angry at Francie anymore. I was just sad at what I had to do next. I'm sure you can see why I had to do it. I had no choice. I turned back to Francie, who had still not moved.

I was almost all blackness now. I was almost gone. Mr. Grossman could no longer see me. Only Francie could see me. Francie could always see me. But she wasn't looking.

I had only one thing left to do.

I took my hand from my pocket and flipped the thing I'd held onto the conference table. I looked back at her and saw her staring down at it, astonished recognition registering in her eyes. She looked up at me one more time, confused and amazed. She began to burn. She was brighter than I had ever seen her.

Then Mr. Grossman saw the thing, too. He reached down and looked at it, unimpressed. "Well, it's worth at least three dollars," he said. He laid it back on the table and punched in the last number. The green LED display rolled over to $501.31. The tape crunched out one more number.

"This is the part of my job that I love," Mr. Grossman said. He chuckled. "Sweetie, I think we're going to have to take a little trip down to the station."

Francie wasn't listening. If Mr. Grossman had looked down at the table, he would have seen that the thing he'd just dropped there had disappeared. Francie had swallowed it. He didn't notice. "Whatever," Francie said, suddenly uncaring. She stood and patted her skirt down. She ran her fingers through her hair and even though it had been sprayed hard in place, it fell around her shoulders as she touched it and kept on falling until it was at her ankles and then was gone, leaving only a burning crown of thorny light at her bare, smooth skull. She turned to me.

"You can go now," she said, without anger. Francie was past anger now. She was something past girl. Francie had completed the transformation she'd been working on since I'd met her; she was a different body now, an all-new person cobbled together from the trinkets she'd stolen over the course of a long and criminal year. Rhinestones where her eyes had been, a paperweight heart. A soul from Claire's Boutique.

I hesitated. I had done what I had wanted to do. I didn't regret it, but still. I wanted to kiss her good-bye. She turned away from me and back to Mr. Grossman, presenting her wrists. "Do you have to handcuff me?" she asked him. He just snorted.

"Francie," I said. But I had been forgotten. Francie was so bright that I had to squint to see her now.

So I went. I walked out of the office, down the long corridor, and back up the stairs to resurface in a mall that I no longer recognized. *Fearless,* I could hear my brother saying. *You are, like, so fearless.* And he was right. I was not scared. I was not sad; I was not even curious to know what would happen next. I knew what would happen.

But the mall was no place for me anymore. Halogen track lights, fake trees, all that *stuff* everywhere. It was all useless to me now. I was headed for the bus—not the J-12, but a bus of my own, a bus that would rumble on beyond the creek and through the city, out past circles and circles of suburbs, and farther, to stop finally where the doors would hiss and swing open into the place that I would consider most perfect. A place I could not name or picture yet but one that I knew existed. I no longer owed my allegiance to Francie, or Jesse, or Liz, or Max, or anyone. I was loyal now only to where I was going: a kingdom of one, a boundless, uncluttered world where I could stand under open sky and stretch out my arms and touch nothing; a place where I belonged to no one and nothing belonged to me.

And though Francie would not be coming along, I owed her a debt of gratitude. She had led me to this place. She knew my ultimate destination. Maybe she'd known what she was doing all along.

Francie had wanted to be the sun. Well, Francie was going to live forever. She could go ahead and be the sun. There's only room for one in any solar system anyway—and talk about your lack of subtlety. It didn't matter; I was something finer, more mysterious. Complicated. I had swallowed, like, this pill of nothingness. I had absence coursing through my veins.

I was a shadow, a shadow, a shadow.

Chapter Twenty-eight

Well? Are you laughing?

ABOUT THE AUTHOR

Bennett Madison learned everything he knows about shoplifting from working at the Gap, where his talent with a price gun earned him the esteemed title of Markdown Specialist, and he learned everything he knows about blondes from attending Sarah Lawrence College, where his four years of lackluster study failed to earn him a diploma. He has spent time as a phone psychic, a receptionist, and a layabout, and his greatest unfulfilled ambition is either to go on *Survivor* or to write X-Men comic books. He lives in New York City. You can visit him online at www.bennettmadison.net.